The Bigfoot Society

A Portland Paranormal Story
Season One

Z.B. Wagman

Robert Eversmann

The Bigfoot Society
A Portland Paranormal Story
www.portlandparanormalpodcast.com

Published by Deep Overstock
Copyright © 2023 by Z.B. Wagman
ISBN: 9781949127393

Cover art by Viviann Ruiz

The Bigfoot Society

Portland
Paranormal
PODCAST

Cast of Characters

SASHA KETCHUM, (30s) missing person.
MARK LANGLEY, (30s) Sasha's best friend.
PATTERSON KETCHUM (mid-30s) Sasha's older brother.
CHARLOTTE "CHARLIE" CHARLESTON, (mid-30s) Sasha's
girlfriend.
ANNIE CHARLESTON, (50s) Charlie's aunt.
JACKO, (50s) Annie's boyfriend.
DETECTIVE MOSBLEY, a detective with the Portland Police
Department.
COREY, (16) the high school mascot.
HANS, an erstwhile birdwatcher.
FRANZ, an erstwhile birdwatcher.
DOCTOR VON BRON, a professor at Portland State
University.
RANGER KENDRA, head ranger in Forest Park.
BERT, Patterson's old friend.
DOCTOR RAHUL CHAKRABARTI, mortician.

Original Cast

The Bigfoot Society premiered on Wednesday, August 2nd,
2023 as the first season of the Portland Paranormal
podcast with the following cast:

SASHA KETCHUM, Simon Lang
MARK LANGLEY, Z.B. Wagman
PATTERSON KETCHUM, Robert Eversmann
CHARLOTTE "CHARLIE" CHARLSTON, Angela van Epps
ANNIE CHARLESTON, Denise Saunders
JACKO, Blaine Ross
DETECTIVE MOSBLEY, Andrew Hatz
HANS, Ryan Sprinkle
FRANZ, Z.B. Wagman
COREY, Viviann Ruiz
DOCTOR VON BRON, Mickey Collins
RANGER KENDRA, Haley Bennet
BERT, Michael Santiago
DOCTOR RAHUL CHAKRABARTI, Alexander Carnes
OTHER VOICES provided by Aimee Bennet, Hannah Collins,
and Justin Wagman

Episode 1

Are You There, Sasha?

SCENE 1.

PATTERSON: You good?

MARK: Yeah, I guess.

PATTERSON: Okay...Whenever you're ready.

A LONG PAUSE FOLLOWED BY A SHARP INTAKE OF AIR FROM MARK AS HE READIES HIMSELF.

MARK: Okay. Go for it.

PATTERSON: Hello. If you're listening to this, our friend Sasha has gone missing, and we need your help.

MARK: He went for a night hike in Forest Park three days ago and no one's heard from him since.

PATTERSON: I know you're going to ask: "why haven't we gone to the cops?" Well, we have--

MARK: (INTERRUPTING) Assholes.

PATTERSON: --and they've basically said that there's nothing they can do.

MARK: They said that he's probably out with an
               ex-girlfriend or something. But I know
               something is wrong. He hasn't called or
               texted...his phone goes straight to
               voicemail. It's so unlike him.

PATTERSON: Basically, the cops won't listen to us--

MARK: Assholes.

PATTERSON: --that's why we're reaching out to you.
               We need to know if any of you were in
               Forest Park the evening of September 4th.
               Did you see Sasha? He's about six-two,
               one-twenty pounds--

MARK: One-thirty-five. God he'd hate that we're
               doing this.

PATTERSON: With brown hair and a sort of scruffy
               goatee.

MARK: He was wearing lime green running shorts
               and a Rage Against the Machine tee.

PATTERSON: He was probably on the Wildwood trail
               from Newberry.

MARK: No. We usually start at Germantown Road.

PATTERSON: Oh yeah? Why weren't you with him that
               night?

MARK: We stopped running together a couple
             weeks ago.

PATTERSON: So he's just been running alone every
             night?

MARK: I…I guess.

<u>AWKWARD PAUSE.</u>

PATTERSON: Okay, let's take a step back. For our
             listeners, I'm Sasha's older brother,
             Patterson. And Mark here is his best
             friend.

MARK: We met in middle school. And have been
             together ever since.

PATTERSON: That's just because you keep mooching off
             him.

MARK: We both work for him. He's done
             everything for us. And we just want to
             find him.

PATTERSON: So, if any of you have seen my little
             brother, please let us know. Keep
             listening for more details. We'll keep
             you informed of anything we find out.

SCENE 2.

PATTERSON: Hi everyone, it's me Patterson. Um, so I'm the one editing these together and this seems like as good a time as any to play our...interview? Um, our phone call with the local police. Spoilers, they don't have much to say.

THERE'S AN OBVIOUS CHANGE IN AUDIO QUALITY.

DET. MOSBLEY: This is detective Mosbley. How can I help you?

MARK: Do you know how long we've been waiting?

DET. MOSBLEY: I'm sorry. As you can imagine, we have a need to prioritize our response around here.

PATTERSON: That's what I told him. Thank you for taking the time, Detective.

DET. MOSBLEY: We do our best. Now, how can I help you gentlemen?

MARK: Forty-five minutes.

DET. MOSBLEY: Excuse me?

MARK: We've been waiting forty-five minutes.

PATTERSON: Mark.

MARK: No. My best friend Sasha is missing, and

              we've had to wait forty-five fucking

              minutes to report it.

DET. MOSBLEY: Like I said, I was dealing with an

              emergency.

MARK: *This* is an emergency.

PATTERSON: No, it's not.

MARK: What?

PATTERSON: I just mean that he's missing. It's not

              like someone's been killed.

MARK: The first 72 hours are the most

              important, Patterson.

PATTERSON: But he's not dead.

MARK: That we know of.

DET. MOSBLEY: Okay okay, you two. Why don't we take a

              breath and start from the beginning.

PATTERSON: (SIGHING) My brother is missing.

MARK: He went for a hike in forest park and

              never came back.

DET. MOSBLEY: He's not one of those Society weirdos, is

              he?

MARK: What? Uh...

PATTERSON: No. He didn't believe any shit like
                 that.

MARK: The what? He just said that he needed
                 some air.

DET. MOSBLEY: Good, good. Always a pain to deal with.
                 You said this happened three days ago?

PATTERSON: Yeah.

DET. MOSBLEY: And have you checked in with his friends,
                 girlfriend...?

MARK: We're his friends.

DET. MOSBLEY: Girlfriend?

MARK: I… I don't think he was seeing any one.

DET. MOSBLEY: Look, he probably met someone at a bar,
                 got caught up in a new thing.

PATTERSON: (LAUGHING) No way. Sasha couldn't make
                 that happen.

DET. MOSBLEY: Give it another day or two and he'll come
                 up for air. We see it all the time.

MARK: And what, we should just sit around with
                 our thumbs up our asses until then?
                 Aren't you going to do anything?

DET. MOSBLEY: Sir, there's nothing we can do at this
                 time.

MARK: You could, I dunno, walk the trail he

                disappeared on. That would be something.

DET. MOSBLEY: *That* would be a waste of manpower.

MARK: Do anything then.

PATTERSON: Mark! I'm sorry officer.

DET. MOSBLEY: It's okay. Tensions can run high in a

                situation like this. I promise he'll show

                up in a couple of days. If there's

                nothing else, you two have a good day.

                HANGS UP PHONE.

MARK: Damn it!

SCENE 3.

PATTERSON: So... We're out hiking Forest Park at dusk because Mark has gone crazy.

MARK: (YELLING FROM AFAR) Because no one else will do anything.

PATTERSON: We've been hiking for...an hour? And it's freezing. With no sign of Sasha.

BUSHES RUSTLE AS MARK DRAWS NEAR.

MARK: Do you think we missed something?

PATTERSON: If I say yes, will we turn around?

MARK: No.

SILENCE EXCEPT FOOTSTEPS.

PATTERSON: My arm's killin' me. Do you really think we're going to find something?

MARK: At least we're looking.

PATTERSON: Yeah.

MARK: He'd do it if it was us.

PATTERSON: (A LITTLE DOUBTING) yeah…

MARK: You know he would.

               SILENCE.

MARK: He hasn't told you about anything, has

               he? Like the cop was saying?

PATTERSON: (PAUSE) Well...no. No.

MARK: You sure?

PATTERSON: Yeah. He would've told us if he had a

               girlfriend.

MARK: That's what I thought. I just...I thought

               maybe he'd been acting strange lately.

               SILENCE.

PATTERSON: Strange how?

MARK: Like sneaking around, or something? Going

               out at night. Like...

PATTERSON: Like he was seeing someone?

MARK: I dunno maybe.

               SILENCE. A SMALL BROOK BABBLES.

PATTERSON: (SHUTTERS) Can we go home now?

MARK: Just a little longer. We've still got

               some light.

PATTERSON: But we'll be hiking back in the dark.

MARK: So?

PATTERSON: I-I don't want to be in the woods in the

               dark. Forest Park is-

MARK: Just a little further, Patterson. Don't

                 be a baby.

                 SILENCE. THE BROOK DRAWS NEAR.

MARK: I'm going to check those bushes.

                 BUSHES RUSTLE AS MARK LEAVES PATH.

PATTERSON: (SIGH) Whatever you say Mark.

                 FOLLOW PATTERSON FOR A MOMENT.

PATTERSON: Let's get this over with.

                 THERE'S A SMALL SPLASH AS SOMETHING IS

                 DROPPED IN STREAM.

PATTERSON: (YELLING) Find anything?

MARK: Not yet.

                 SPLASHING AS PATTERSON WADES IN.

MARK: (YELLING) Anything?

PATTERSON: No. Wait! I think I see something in the

                 water.

                 MORE SPLASHING.

MARK: (COMING CLOSER) What is it?

PATTERSON: Dunno. Almost there. (PAUSE) It's a… It's

                 a phone. I think it's Sasha's phone.

MARK: Let me see!

                 SPLASHING AS MARK ENTERS THE WATER.

MARK: It's the right model! Did we do it? Did

                 we find something? (YELLING) SASHA!!

PATTERSON: What?

MARK: (YELLING) SASHA!

PATTERSON: Stop that.

MARK: What if he's hurt? (YELLING) SASHA! CAN

              YOU HEAR ME?

PATTERSON: Stop it. He's not here.

MARK: You don't know that. (YELLING) SASHA

              WE'RE COMING.

PATTERSON: Mark, stop. Look around, he's not here.

MARK: But he could be hurt.

PATTERSON: There's no sign of anything. No blood. No

              struggle. And it's dark. If we wander off

              the path *we* could get lost.

MARK: But he's here. I know he's here.

PATTERSON: Look, we don't even know if it's his

              phone.

MARK: So turn it on.

PATTERSON: What?

MARK: Turn it on.

PATTERSON: It's wet.

MARK: Just do it.

PATTERSON: (SIGHING) Fine.

              PHONE NOISES.

PATTERSON: Do you know this passcode?

MARK: Don't you? (PAUSE) 7782824.

PATTERSON: It's open.

MARK: It's his! (YELLING) SASHA!

PATTERSON: He's not here.

MARK: SASHA!

               PHONE DINGS. NEW MESSAGE.

PATTERSON: A text?

MARK: What's it say? Who's it from?

PATTERSON: "What happened to you?"

MARK: What? Who's it from?

PATTERSON: Charlie?

MARK: Who is Charlie?

Episode 2

Go Bigfoots!

SCENE 1.

MARK: To all of you who have helped get the word out about Sasha, thank you. We are so grateful for all the support. There's been no sign of him yet but in the meantime, we have a lot to figure out.

PATTERSON: We do? Like what?

MARK: Charlie. Sasha's phone. What else?!

PATTERSON: Calm down, dude.

MARK: Calm down? It's been three days since we found our missing friend's phone and we've done nothing about it!

PATTERSON: And you're not helping anything. We need to think about this.

MARK: What's there to think about?!

PATTERSON: Well, do you think this Charlie had anything to do with Sasha's disappearance?

MARK: No. I mean, maybe. How should I know?

PATTERSON: What did the text say?

MARK: 'What happened to you?' But then I texted
               back--

PATTERSON: You texted back?!

MARK: Yeah, I wanted to know what was going on.

PATTERSON: What did you say?!

MARK: 'Sorry, lost track of time. Do you wanna
               meet up?'

PATTERSON: Why would you say that?

MARK: Because I want to know who this person
               is.

PATTERSON: So, what's your plan? Meet them at a
               coffee shop and say 'You don't know me,
               but have you seen Sasha. Oh, FYI I'm the
               one who's been texting you.'

MARK: It's not a bad plan.

PATTERSON: Oh god.

MARK: But then he wanted to meet at the game!

PATTERSON: What game?

MARK: Umm. I don't know.

PATTERSON: (SIGHS) None of the pros are playing this
               week.

MARK: The Thorns? Timbers? The Blazers?

PATTERSON: None of them.

MARK: Shit. Should I ask Charlie?

PATTERSON: Don't you think Sasha would already know

              which game.

MARK: Shit.

              <u>LONG PAUSE.</u>

PATTERSON: You know who is playing? Our old high

              school soccer team.

MARK: What would Sasha be doing there?

PATTERSON: I dunno. But I bet I'm right.

MARK: Really? He hated the place.

PATTERSON: It's not so bad.

MARK: It's not Sasha's thing.

PATTERSON: What's your better idea?

SCENE 2.

<u>CORNY PEP BAND MUSIC.</u>

MARK: This is humiliating.

CORY: (FROM A DISTANCE THROUGH A MEGAPHONE)
             WE'VE GOT!

CROWD: (FROM A DISTANCE) NO SHOES!

MARK: I hate this place. Why would Sasha be
             here?

PATTERSON: Reliving the glory days.

MARK: Sasha didn't have glory days.

PATTERSON: Then why does he still wear his class
             ring?

MARK: Because he's a loser?

PATTERSON: Watch it! I've still got mine.

MARK: I guess it runs in the family.

CORY: (FROM A DISTANCE) WE'VE GOT!

CROWD: (FROM A DISTANCE) BIG FEET!

MARK: (IN A DAZE) Jesus...

PATTERSON: Let's go find a seat. Bert usually saves
             me one in the boosters' section.

MARK: Boosters section?

PATTERSON: Yeah… I come to a lot of these I guess.

              CUT TAPE.

              START TAPE, CROWD NOISE IN BACKGROUND.

MARK: How are we gonna find this guy?

PATTERSON: (DISTRACTED) Dunno. Do you think Sanchez

              is going to start tonight?

MARK: Who?

PATTERSON: Sanchez. Our star striker.

MARK: What are you talking about?

PATTERSON: Hey, there's Bert. BERT!

BERT: Look who decided to show his face.

PATTERSON: Don't even get started ya big fur ball.

BERT: Did you hear that Sanchez is still out?

PATTERSON: No way.

BERT: They're starting Williams instead.

PATTERSON: Williams?! You've got to be kidding me.

              The kid has two left feet.

BERT: And can't go a mile without fainting.

PATTERSON: We're screwed.

BERT: Totally screwed.

MARK: Patterson?

PATTERSON: (DISTRACTED) What?

MARK: Charlie?

PATTERSON: Oh yeah. Hey Bert, you ever seen a fellow

                named Charlie around here?

BERT: That one of the JV players?

PATTERSON: No clue.

BERT: Can't say it rings a bell.

MARK: What about Sasha?

BERT: Sasha?

PATTERSON: My brother. Skinny, AV kid a couple years

                below us.

BERT: No clue. Sorry dude.

PATTERSON: Ah well.

CORY: Give me a B!

CROWD, PATTERSON, BERT: B!

MARK: Hey, what happened to Sassy?

                <u>CUT TAPE.</u>

                <u>START TAPE, CROWD NOISE IN BACKGROUND.</u>

PATTERSON: Hey Cory. This is Mark. Mark, this is

                Cory.

CORY: Hi Mark.

PATTERSON: Cory, why are you dressed like that?

CORY: I'm the mascot here at Gimlin High School

                and...

MARK: Do you mind describing your outfit? We're

                recording for a podcast.

CORY: Um...

PATTERSON: Well?

CORY: Um, I'm in a dirty soccer practice

               uniform that one of the guys gave me and

               I've glued, um, hair to my face.

PATTERSON: Whose hair?

MARK: (INTERRUPTING) Why did you glue hair to

               your face?

CORY: I'm a little afraid to speak negativity

               out loud on account of words having so

               much power and-

PETERSON: Cory.

CORY: And I don't really want it to come true,

               you see, and-

PATTERSON: Out with it, Cory.

CORY: I- uh, it's my brother's hair.

MARK: Where is the Bigfoot suit?

PATTERSON: Under your bed?

CORY: (GULP) I think Sassy the Sasquatch has

               been stolen. I had her last week and then

               poof gone.

MARK: I don't think it just vanished.

CORY: I dunno man. I took her off for a second

               to do...something. And then she vanished.

PATTERSON: Did something?

CORY: (MUMBLES)

MARK: What?

CORY: I maybe lit a joint?

              <u>CUT TAPE.</u>

              <u>START TAPE, CROWD NOISE IN BACKGROUND.</u>

MARK: Didn't think they sold beer at high
              school soccer games.

PATTERSON: Or sold weed to high schoolers. I like
              Cory but damn. Smoking before games?
              Losing the suit?

              <u>CHEERING FROM THE CROWD.</u>

              NUT MEG! You see that shit?

              (PATTERSON JOINS CHEERING) Wooo!

              Ow! Damn, shoulder still hurts like a…

MARK: Let's get this over with. I'm texting
              him.

              <u>TEXTING W/ IPHONE CLICK ON.</u>

              (TEXTING) Hey, I'm here. Smiley face
              emoji.

PATTERSON: What are you doing?

MARK: I'm finding Charlie.

PATTERSON: Can't it wait till half time?

MARK: Patterson. This is _the_ whole reason we're

                 here!

PATTERSON: I mean, this is _A_ reason we're here.

                 <u>IPHONE MESSAGE RECEIVED.</u>

PATTERSON: What's it say?

MARK: "The usual spot. Where are you?"

PATTERSON: The usual spot?

MARK: Has Sasha been coming to these games?

PATTERSON: I would have seen him.

MARK: How should I know what "the usual spot"

                 is?

PATTERSON: Because you're Sasha, remember? Give me

                 that. (SOUND OF PHONE CHANGING HANDS.

                 TEXTING.) 'Getting a beer.'

                 <u>MESSAGE SENT.</u>

MARK: But I just got a beer.

PATTERSON: Well now you can get another.

                 <u>IPHONE MESSAGE RECEIVED.</u>

PATTERSON: "Bring me one." Shit.

MARK: What are you doing?

PATTERSON: (TYPING) 'Meet me? Hands full, got

                 popcorn too.'

                 <u>MESSAGE SENT.</u>

MARK: You better not have messed this up.

PATTERSON: "Fine. But you're paying."

MARK: Two beers and a large popcorn.

CASHIER: That all?

MARK: Ooh and a twizzler.

CASHIER: $27.50

MARK: Really?

MARK: Any sign yet?

PATTERSON: (GRUNTS NONCOMMITTALLY)

MARK: You know how much they charge here?

PATTERSON: That's why you paid.

MARK: Asshole.

               Is that him?

PATTERSON: That's Rodger Simms. He was a couple

               years before me.

MARK: Oh.

PATTERSON: What did you do?

MARK: Asked where he was.

MARK: "I don't see you." Now what?

PATTERSON: Give me that. (TEXTING) "I'm done. I'm

                 not playing this game anymore."

MARK: What?! Don't send that. Seriously. Don't

                 send that.

                 <u>SENT MESSAGE SOUND.</u>

MARK: Dammit Patterson. Come on, give it back

                 to me.

PATTERSON: No way. I'm not messing around with this

                 stupid Charlie stuff any-

                 <u>PHYSICAL STRUGGLE.</u>

PATTERSON: Ow, dammit Mark. My arm. That hurts like

                 a-

                 <u>PHONE RINGING.</u>

PATTERSON: Wait. You're calling him?!

                 <u>AUDIBLE RINGTONE NEARBY.</u>

MARK: I hear him nearby.

                 <u>ANSWERS PHONE.</u>

MARK: Hello?

                 <u>SAME BACKGROUND NOISE NOW COMING THROUGH</u>

                 <u>PHONE.</u>

CHARLIE: Where the fuck have you been, Sasha? …

                 Hello?

                 <u>CUT TAPE.</u>

30

Episode 3

There's Something You Need to Know about Sasha

SCENE 1.

PATTERSON: Charlotte! It's been so long! I didn't
know you were back in town.

CHARLIE: Oh, uh, hi Patterson. It's been a while.

PATTERSON: Are you back visiting? I'd love to take
you out while you're here. For old time's
sake.

CHARLIE: (DISTRACTED) I've actually moved back.
Got a job teaching freshmen lit.

PATTERSON: Wow, you're teaching here? Crazy.

CHARLIE: Look, Patterson, it was nice to see you
but I'm actually looking for your
brother.

PATTERSON: Do you remember Mark? Hey Mark--it's
Charlotte! (TO CHARLIE) This is Mark
Langley, he was the same year as my
brother. Mark, you remember Charlotte.

MARK: Nice to see you--

CHARLIE: It's Charlie, now.

PATTERSON: What?

MARK: Wait. What?

CHARLIE: I go by Charlie now. Patterson, have you

              seen your brother?

MARK: You're Charlie?

CHARLIE: Yes, I-- He's supposed to be meeting

              me...

MARK: You're who I've been texting?

CHARLIE: What?

MARK: Why were you texting Sasha?

CHARLIE: Wait. Is Sasha here with you guys?

MARK: No. He--

CHARLIE: Who have I been texting with?

MARK: Um, me. Look--

CHARLIE: Assholes. Did Sasha put you up to this?

MARK: No, he's not--

PATTERSON: Why didn't you text me?

CHARLIE: What?

PATTERSON: We used to be close.

CHARLIE: Look. Tell me where Sasha is.

MARK: We don't know!

              <u>PAUSE.</u>

              He's missing.

CHARLIE: What.

MARK: He's been missing for six days.

CHARLIE: Not possible.

PATTERSON: It is.

CHARLIE: He just texted me yesterday.

MARK: Umm.

CHARLIE: Shit. (BREATH TO CALM SELF DOWN) Ok, is
              there a reason, you're, you know,
              pretending to be Sasha?

PATTERSON: You barely knew Sasha.

MARK: That's not true, Patterson-I've seen the
              texts…

CHARLIE: You're both assholes.

MARK: When did you last see him?

CHARLIE: I don't know. We were supposed to meet
              up. Look, what is this about? Where is
              he?

PATTERSON: Meet up?

MARK: When?

CHARLIE: Six days ago. But he never showed. I
              thought he was blowing me off.

MARK: Oh.

PATTERSON: What were you doing?

CHARLIE: Is that any of your business?

PATTERSON: Yes.

CHARLIE: Screw you.

MARK: Look, we're just trying to find Sasha.

CHARLIE: Maybe next time, you don't pretend to be

               someone's boyfriend. I'm out.

SCENE 2.

<u>INTERIOR OF A CAR.</u>

MARK: So. Charlie.

PATTERSON: What about her?

MARK: Weird seeing her again.

PATTERSON: I guess.

MARK: Weird Sasha never mentioned her.

               <u>PAUSE.</u>

PATTERSON: Yeah.

MARK: I wonder what else he hasn't mentioned.

               <u>SILENCE.</u>

               Has he ever said...?

PATTERSON: He didn't say shit, Mark.

MARK: Okay...

PATTERSON: No. It's not okay. Secret girlfriends,
               secret late-night meetings in the woods,
               what's next? Why'd he keep so much from
               us?

MARK: It sucks.

PATTERSON: It more than sucks. He's an asshole.

MARK: Patterson.

PATTERSON: He was. A big hairy asshole.

MARK: Patterson, stop.

PATTERSON: No. I'm his brother. He shouldn't keep

             secrets from me.

MARK: I'm his friend, he didn't tell me.

PATTERSON: It's different.

MARK: Why?

PATTERSON: It just is.

MARK: Because you used to have a thing for

             Charlie?

PATTERSON: No. Yes--we dated like for a month senior

             year.

MARK: You did?

PATTERSON: Yeah, went on a couple of dates.

MARK: How many?

PATTERSON: Does it matter?

MARK: Yes.

PATTERSON: Two. We went on two dates and Sasha knew

             it. He should have known better.

MARK: Patterson.

PATTERSON: What?

MARK: You weren't dating.

PATTERSON: I just told you--

MARK: Two dates is not dating.

PATTERSON: Yes, it is.

MARK: Okay, then she dumped you.

PATTERSON: She didn't--I did the--No. That's not

               what happened.

MARK: Because you weren't dating?

PATTERSON: Shut up, Mark.

MARK: That's what I thought.

PATTERSON: At least I didn't have to wait till

               college to get it wet.

MARK: Gross.

PATTERSON: I'm just telling the truth.

MARK: You're just being a dick. What do we do

               now?

PATTERSON: I dunno. Sleep on it?

MARK: I guess.

SCENE 3.

<u>IN THE STUDIO.</u>

MARK: Okay, so we've both had a little time to
             process yesterday's news...

PATTERSON: You mean we slept one off and are just
             now getting over the hangover.

MARK: Are you hungover? I know I didn't sleep
             much but I wasn't drinking. I mean, I've
             been a little too focused on Sasha.

PATTERSON: Will you give it a rest?

MARK: No, listen. I've been thinking about our
             evidence.

PATTERSON: We don't have evidence. The cops said so.

MARK: That was almost a week ago! Actually, we
             should probably call them for an update.

PATTERSON: No. We have nothing to update them on.

MARK: This is what I'm trying to say: we know

               Sasha disappeared a week ago in Forest

               Park. We found his phone along the

               Wildwood Trail. That was also the day he

               was supposed to meet Charlie.

PATTERSON: His secret girlfriend.

MARK: Exactly! I've been going through their

               texts--

PATTERSON: Anything kinky?

MARK: No. But I figured out that she was going

               to meet him at the park that night.

PATTERSON: Wait, what?

MARK: Yes! So, if he never showed, and the last

               time either of us saw him that day was

               4pm, then we've got a window.

PATTERSON: We've got more than that.

MARK: What do you mean?

PATTERSON: She was supposed to meet him in the park.

MARK: Yeah.

PATTERSON: And we know he made it to the park

               because of his phone.

MARK: But she said she never saw him.

               <u>PAUSE.</u>

               Could she be lying?

PATTERSON: Maybe.

MARK: But why would she lie?

PATTERSON: Maybe she knows more than she's let on.

MARK: You think?

PATTERSON: It's worth asking.

MARK: Yeah. It is.

                 SILENCE. A PHONE RINGS.

MARK: Shit.

PATTERSON: What is it?

MARK: It's Sasha's. It's her.

PATTERSON: What?

MARK: She's calling!

PATTERSON: So pickup.

MARK: And say what?

PATTERSON: Give it to me.

MARK: No. I'll do it. (DEEP BREATH) Hello?

CHARLIE: Mark?

MARK: Yeah.

CHARLIE: Listen. I'm sorry. Don't get me wrong,
                 I'm still pissed at you.

MARK: Sure.

CHARLIE: Like who pretends to be somebody's
                 missing boyfriend?

MARK: Uh, yeah.

CHARLIE: But I also really want to find him and it

            seems like you guys might know

            something.

MARK: We might.

CHARLIE: I know some things too. We were involved

            in something. Sasha said he didn't want

            you to know, but I'm really worried.

            There's something you need to know about

            Sasha...

SCENE 4.

<u>CUT. DOOR OPENS AS CHARLIE COMES IN AND PUTS BAG ON COUNTER.</u>

MARK: Hey, Charlie I'm really sorry.

CHARLIE: Save it Mark.

MARK: I didn't know who you were. I just want to find him.

CHARLIE: Look, I don't care what you want. I have information. You have information. I'm here so we can compare notes and hopefully find Sasha. Alright?

MARK: Alright.

PATTERSON: Hey! Charlotte! Nice to see ya.

CHARLIE: (DEEP SIGH) Just. Ok, here it is. I have a voice message from Sasha. It's… weird. I haven't shown it to anyone else. It's _really_ weird. Are you ready?

MARK & PATTERSON: (SOUNDS OF ASSENT)

<u>A VOICE RECORDING. FOREST SOUNDS IN THE BACKGROUND.</u>

SASHA: Hey, it's Sasha! Sorry I'm running late;
            I had trouble getting away from
            Patterson. I think he knows what we've
            been up to. I could see it in his eyes.
            He called me fantasy-prone. I mean- am I?
            Why am I out alone in the woods at night?
            I mean, what the hell is wrong with me?
            (TENSION LAUGH) Anyway, I'm in the park
            now--maybe ten minutes out? I've been
            thinking a lot about this...and us. I
            feel like I'm back in high school--not
            that we had anything to do with each
            other in high school. You were, are, so
            out of my league. And now? Now we're
            together because I believe in- in...?
            (TENSION LAUGH) See, fantasy prone.
            PAUSE. FOOTSTEPS IN THE WOODS.
            Shit sorry. I don't mean to dredge up the
            past. I've just been thinking a lot about
            it lately. About how much those early
            relationships can define us. Not _us_ us.
            I mean us as in people. Like, just the
            opposite of _us_. Because we're good,
            right? We are good.

But like Mark and Patterson have been in my life since...practically the beginning. And it used to be so good but lately I just feel like I'm going through the motions with them. Like maybe they're pulling away. Or I am?

Since you and I started-- Since I know you believe- I mean, ever since the night I saw you at that meeting, I've felt different. Like I'm in the middle of some change I can't avoid. (PAUSE) You showed how to take the next step forward. And I can't thank you enough for that, I just… god this is harder than I expected. It's been great. It really has been… But that next step... There's so much at stake. Can I really trust it?

Shit. What was that?

(OUT) Uh, Charlie is that you?

This isn't funny. Charlie? I… I… see you
behind the tree. Stop this.

What are you doing—

MARK: Oh my god. Was Sasha shot?

PATTERSON: Are you kidding me? (POORLY IMITATES
             SCREAM). That for sure was a hoax.

CHARLIE: That's what I thought. It sounds like—

PATTERSON: It sounds like he's breaking up with
             you.

CHARLIE: Yeah. But then... Well, I assumed the
             scream was you two.

PATTERSON: What?

CHARLIE: Here.

SASHA: (START) There's so much at sta- (STOP)

CHARLIE: A little more.

SASHA: I… I… see you behind the tree. Stop this.

             PAUSE. RUSTLING

CHARLIE: There we go.

SASHA: What are you doing--

                <u>AN ANIMALISTIC SCREAM. NOISE OF STRUGGLE.</u>

                <u>PHONE IS DROPPED. SILENCE. BRIEF FUMBLING</u>

                <u>OF PHONE. THE LINE GOES DEAD.</u>

CHARLIE: I thought you two were helping Sasha

                break up with me, but then, last night,

                at the game, you looked so shocked. Like

                you really had no idea where Sasha was.

                But-I'm just overthinking it aren't I? It

                is just a joke. If Sasha doesn't want to

                see me, that's fine, whatever-

MARK: We haven't seen Sasha in over a week.

                That wasn't us.

CHARLIE: Oh.

MARK: What did he mean pulling away?

CHARLIE: I don't know. Sasha seems down sometimes.

                He obsesses about certain things. They go

                around and around in his head. But I

                don't know. He talks about you two a lot.

                He says you and Patterson-

PATTERSON: Hold on hold on hold on. Wait a minute.
                What's going on here? Sasha was going to
                come and meet you, right? He calls you.
                He sees you hiding behind a tree like
                some ax-killer. Let me see your phone.

CHARLIE: What-

PATTERSON: Whoop, thanks. Great, still unlocked.

CHARLIE: Hey!

SASHA: (START) What are you- (STOP)

CHARLIE: I wasn't-

PATTERSON: Shh.

SASHA: (START) This isn't funny. Charlie? I… I…
                see you behind the tree. Stop this.
                (STOP)

CHARLIE: I never saw Sasha that night.

PATTERSON: "This isn't funny. Charlie." Don't put
                this on us. You were the one Sasha was
                out there to meet.

CHARLIE: No, I didn't-

PATTERSON: Shall I play it again?

CHARLIE: I mean, yes. Yes, I was out there. But
                when he called it went straight to
                voicemail. I had no signal, because I was
                still at the top of the woods waiting for
                Sasha.

PATTERSON: Uh huh… Phone signal. That's your alibi?

CHARLIE: We were in two different places. And I
                mean, why would I show you this? If I was
                out there. If I hurt Sasha. Does it make
                sense I'd show you this voicemail now?

PATTERSON: So… have you taken this to the cops?

MARK: Wait, what?

CHARLIE: I haven't told them.

MARK: Why not?

CHARLIE: I just… it's weird okay. I thought he was
                breaking up with me.

MARK: By meeting you in the woods?

CHARLIE: But he didn't. He didn't meet me in the
                woods, okay? You weren't there. You
                didn't stand around for an hour in the
                cold waiting for him.

MARK: Yeah. But you could've still gone to the
                cops.

CHARLIE: And say what? "I was waiting to meet my
                boyfriend out in the woods. He didn't
                show up but he left me this joke
                voicemail. I promise I didn't kill him."

MARK: I get it.

CHARLIE: Great.

MARK: So… Can I ask, why were you meeting Sasha
                in the woods?

CHARLIE: We had a… thing.

MARK: A thing?

CHARLIE: Yeah, a thing. An event. Every First
                Sunday. No? Well, Sasha started coming to
                them a few months ago. It's a sort of
                gathering of like-minded people.

PATTERSON: Sounds kinky.

CHARLIE: No. Not like that. It's a sort of social
                club.

MARK: A club?

CHARLIE: It's a little outside the ordinary.

MARK: How outside the ordinary?

CHARLIE: Um—

PATTERSON: Just spit it out.

CHARLIE: (DEFINITIVE SIGH) It'll be easier to show
                you…

<u>CUT TAPE.</u>

<u>CUT TAPE.</u>

Episode 4

The Society

SCENE 1.

MARK: (WHISPERING) Where are we?

PATTERSON: Isn't this the old PSU auditorium?

CHARLIE: (WHISPERING) Shh, they're in the middle of a presentation. Come on. This way. We can sit in the back.

ANNIE: This discussion is ridiculous. Whatever you think you saw, I assure you, you saw no such thing.

DR. VON BRON: If they saw _anything_ out there, that's a pretty good indication of danger.

LARGER RUMBLE FROM THE AUDIENCE.

ANNIE: (RAISING) People think they see things all the time. How much credibility will we lose as a society if we brazenly declare we've seen Bigfoot when we've seen nothing at all.

PATTERSON: (WHISPERING) Did she just say Bigfoot?

DR. VON BRON: (DISGUSTED) Hans and Franz saw him!

HANS: Yes. It is true! We saw him!

FRANZ: With our own eyes!

               GROWING HUBBUB IN THE AUDIENCE.

ANNIE: (INSISTENT) Really? When did you see him?

               In the day or at night?

HANS: At night.

ANNIE: And how close were you? Would you say

               about our distance right now? Maybe

               fifteen feet?

FRANZ: Maybe.

ANNIE: Maybe. So you can't say clearly. It could

               have been fifteen or fifty or five

               hundred feet. You don't recall?

HANS: Perhaps it was…

ANNIE: And this was at night. Is that correct?

HANS: We smelled him.

ANNIE: You smelled him…? Okay… I'm not spending

               my time on this. The festival is in two

               weeks…

FRANZ: He smelled like mud and like pine!

ANNIE: Like mud and pine. So… Our two members, bird watchers on their own time, smelled the woods at midnight. Are we ready to call the papers?

SERIOUS HUBBUB IN THE AUDIENCE.

ANNIE: Do I have to remind you that the festival is *the* event keeping this society alive? Without the income from the festival, we cannot afford to pay our speakers, we cannot afford to pay our fees for the hunts, we cannot even afford the rent to keep this very roof above our heads! There is no reason at all that we ought to stop or delay or change, in any way, the festival. There is no danger. There is onl-

DR. VON BRON: Safety, Madame President, is something the society has strived for since its inception. If one of our members claim a sighting, we should proceed with caution. And if two of our members claim a sighting…

A HUBBUB ARISES AGAIN!

ANNIE: Did either of you happen to get a picture

                  or catch anything on film? No? Anyone?

                  No?

HANS: Why don't you ask Jacko? He's the one who

                  shot it!

                  A BIG HUBBUB ABUB!

CHARLIE: (WHISPERING) Wait, Jacko shot something?

MARK: (WHISPERING) Who's Jacko?

ANNIE: Order order order. We do not slander

                  members of this society. Jacko, do you

                  have something to share?

JACKO: (COUGHS ON HIS OWN WORDS) I can't... I-I-I

                  mean I didn't...

ANNIE: Jacko didn't shoot anything.

FRANZ: Annie, I heard a gunshot!

ANNIE: (RUBBING HER EYES) You probably heard a

                  car backfiring...

DR. VON BRON: I heard it too. It was not a car

                  backfiring. It was a live round. Jacko if

                  you shot something...

JACKO: I didn't shoot anybody. I didn't. I-

DR. VON BRON: If you saw *anything* which can help us

                  shed light on what's going on in the

                  woods...

JACKO: I-

ANNIE: If someone gets real, definitive proof.

             That is huge. That is outstanding. All

             our work in the society will really mean

             something. But—but if we start

             publicizing something that's a hunch at

             best, our donors will back out. Our

             society will just—end. I'm not taking

             that risk. Now, if you will excuse me.

             I've got a festival to plan. Meeting

             adjourned.

             CHAIR LEGS SCRAPING AMIDST GRUMBLING.

SCENE 2.

<u>HUBBUB OF THE CROWD IN BACKGROUND.</u>

MARK: Charlie, is this society a Bigfoot
            society?

CHARLIE: Ha Ha Ha… Surprise.

PATTERSON: So, did Sasha come to these?

CHARLIE: Yeah, it's how we reconnected.

MARK: I can't believe Sasha believed in- in-

CHARLIE: Well, maybe that's why he never told you.

MARK: What's that mean?

CHARLIE: Maybe he thought you'd judge him.

PATTERSON: You don't... believe in this stuff, do
            you?

CHARLIE: (LYING) No, no. I mean-

PATTERSON: So why do you come?

CHARLIE: Well, I've been doing it forever. My aunt
            has been bringing me here since I was a
            kid. And then, a couple months ago, Sasha
            showed up out of the blue.

PATTERSON: So when you were out in the woods waiting

                 for Sasha?

CHARLIE: Yep.

PATTERSON: You were...

CHARLIE: Looking for Bigfoot.

                 <u>FOOTSTEPS DRAWING CLOSER.</u>

DR. VON BRON: Who's looking for Bigfoot?

CHARLIE: If it isn't the venerable Dr. Von Bron.

DR. VON BRON: Charlie.

CHARLIE: You've made my aunt angry again.

DR. VON BRON: Yes, well. A lot riding on it I suppose.

                 The balance of donor money and human

                 life.

CHARLIE: Do you really think there could be

                 something dangerous out there?

DR. VON BRON: There are dangers out in the woods

                 whether we want them or not.

MARK: And, in Forest Park? Do you think there's

                 something dangerous out there?

DR. VON BRON: May I ask, what is this about?

MARK: Our friend is missing. It's been ten

                 days.

CHARLIE: Last we heard from him he was on his way
                into the woods. I was there waiting for
                him.

DR. VON BRON: And I take it this was the night Hans and
                Franz had a run in with Bigfoot.

CHARLIE: Yeah, the night of the last hunt.

DR. VON BRON: You believe what you want to believe, but
                I believe in what I've seen. And I
                believe he is dangerous. I'd like to
                think your friend is still alive but…

MARK: So he could have gone after Sasha?

DR. VON BRON: It's certainly possible but I wouldn't
                expect for a cognatus to prey on one of
                us-it would have to be exceedingly
                desperate for a food source. Where did
                you say your friend disappeared?

MARK: We found his phone along the Wildwood
                trail in Forest Park.

DR. VON BRON: Hm... We might consider the changing
environment. There have been concerted
construction projects in that area as of
late. I expect those would drive off most
of a cognatus's usual prey. And of course
during the summer, Forest Park has
increased foot traffic driving away even
more potential prey.

PATTERSON: So you're saying that it's a possibility?

DR. VON BRON: I'm saying that, as there is a cognatus
in the area, it may have been starved to
the point of desperation. If your friend
presented a weak enough target, or if he
were simply unlucky to be out alone in
the evening during prime hunting time,
there's a high probability that the
cognatus saw him as viable game.

CHARLIE: In other words, if Bigfoot was hungry
enough, he might have gone after Sasha.

DR. VON BRON: I'm afraid it's not outside the realm of
possibility.

CHARLIE: Oh my god. Sasha.

DR. VON BRON: Look--My sister is a park ranger with
Portland Parks and Recreation. Why don't
you go see her in the morning? Maybe
she's seen something. It's worth stopping
by. She's at the ranger's station in
Forest Park every day. Now, I really must
go. Have a nice evening, kids.

<u>FOOTSTEPS LEAVING.</u>

MARK: You don't think... that they actually saw
something, do you?

CHARLIE: (IMMEDIATELY) Something? Yes.

PATTERSON: But a Bigfoot?

CHARLIE: (LYING) No. No, probably not but...

PATTERSON: But what?

CHARLIE: Nothing. I guess.

<u>FOOTSTEPS DRAWING CLOSER.</u>

JACKO: Charlie. Been a while since you've come
over.

CHARLIE: Jacko! Sorry, I've been a bit busy.

JACKO: With your new boyfriend.

CHARLIE: Have you seen him lately?

JACKO: Not for a couple days.

CHARLIE: Oh...when-

MARK: We heard that you saw something during
                the hunt.

JACKO: Every night's a hunt.

MARK: Oh. Uh, during the Bigfoot hunt last
                weekend?

PATTERSON: Did you see something?

JACKO: I was with your aunt the whole night.

CHARLIE: Okay. So if I ask her...?

JACKO: (GRUNTS)

MARK: We think something happened to Sasha that
                night.

JACKO: Ask your aunt.

FOOTSTEPS DRAWING CLOSER.

ANNIE: Ohh, Charlie. So glad you could make it
                tonight. I wanted to touch base with you
                about the vendor list for the festival.

CHARLIE: Oh, uh, okay. Does it have to be now?

ANNIE: Why? Do you have something more important
                going on?

CHARLIE: Well, uh, this is Mark and Patterson,
                they're friends of Sasha's.

PATTERSON: Actually, I'm his brother.

ANNIE: Oh, is that right? You don't look similar
                at all.

PATTERSON: Yeah, well you can't choose who you're
                related to.

MARK: Do you know anything about Sasha's
                disappearance?

ANNIE: Why would I know anything about that? I
                just assumed he had gotten…well, bored
                with my Charlotte.

CHARLIE: (HURT) Auntie.

ANNIE: I'm sorry, Charlie but it's true. Anyway,
                I've been much too busy to think about
                that.

MARK: Yeah, are these meetings usually
                so…exciting?

ANNIE: Some people are just so full of
                themselves. They believe they can prove
                anything with just a word.

CHARLIE: It's not a big deal.

ANNIE: We're a serious society, you know. And we
                need to maintain that image with the rest
                of the city. Anyway, the world goes on,
                as will the festival. Pleased to meet you
                I'm sure. Jacko are you-oh, you look
                terrible.

JACKO: I'm fine.

PATTERSON: We were just asking Jacko about the night
               of the hunt.

ANNIE: As if we haven't hashed that out enough
               already. I was just on my way home,
               Charlie. Shall I give you a ride?

CHARLIE: I uh… I've got plans with Mark and
               Patterson.

               CUT.

Episode 5

It Was Bigfoot?!

SCENE 1.

<u>WALKING THROUGH WOODS.</u>

MARK: Are we really discussing this?

CHARLIE: Yes.

PATTERSON: (ON HER HEELS) Shouldn't we explore every
            possible option?

MARK: Hello listeners. Charlie, Patterson, and
            Mark here. We're on the way to meet Dr.
            Von Bron's sister, Kendra, the lead
            ranger in Forest Park. (SARCASTIC) And,
            oh, we think Bigfoot is responsible for
            Sasha's disappearance.

CHARLIE: I know you think this is some kind of
            joke but _something_ happened to Sasha.

MARK: But… Bigfoot?

PATTERSON: When are you going to get it, Mark-

               someone killed Sasha. Was it Bigfoot?

               Maybe! That creep at the Society meeting?

               In all likelihood yes! But someone's

               responsible. You can't keep going around

               believing in the best of people.

               SILENCE.

MARK: (MUMBLING) Sasha's not dead.

PATTERSON: What?

MARK: How do you know that Sasha is dead?

PATTERSON: Come on! It's been almost two weeks and

               the best lead we have is that Bigfoot did

               it. Do you really think he's locked in a

               basement somewhere? Grow up, man.

               SILENCE.

CHARLIE: (TRYING TO CLEAR THE AIR) So. Bigfoot?

MARK: Are we really this desperate for a

               suspect?

CHARLIE: Sasha believed.

MARK: Apparently.

PATTERSON: You know what your problem is, Mark? You

               were too close. You were 'such good

               friends' because you're exactly alike.

MARK: That's not fair.

PATTERSON: No? He believed in fairytales and
               Bigfoot. It got him killed. You believe
               that he could be lost in the woods. Be
               careful your fantasies don't kill you
               too.

CHARLIE: Don't be a dick, Patterson.

PATTERSON: I'm just giving him some honest advice.

CHARLIE: And I'm doing the same: quit being such
               an ass.

PATTERSON: Whatever.

               SILENCE. FOOTSTEPS IN THE WOODS.

               CUT TAPE.

SCENE 2.

INDOORS.

RANGER KENDRA: Lost yo-yos. Lost hats. Lost backpacks. Lost coffee mugs.

FRISBEE IS PUT ON THE TABLE.

KENDRA: This is the frisbee of a thirty-five-year-old man who tripped over a gopher hole and broke his clavicle.

METAL BUCKET IS PUT ON THE TABLE.

RANGER KENDRA: These are the remains of an illegal campsite whose owner fell asleep in front of the fire.

FENDER IS PUT ON THE TABLE.

RANGER KENDRA: (GRUNTS) This here's the fender off someone's car who drove down a ravine. The rest of the car's still stuck down there. Any of this what you're looking for?

CHARLIE: Sorry, I think there's been a
                misunderstanding—we're here to ask you
                about some of the dangers associated with
                the park. Your brother suggested we come
                talk to you…

RANGER KENDRA: My brother?!

CHARLIE: Yes. Dr. Von Bron.

RANGER KENDRA: *Hoo*… don't listen to anything my brother
                says. I love the guy, but he is a grade
                'A' nut.

MARK: But Dr. Von Bron mentioned there's been
                construction near Forest Park that could
                be disturbing the animals.

RANGER KENDRA: It's true that Jack Hammers and other
                construction sounds certainly disturb the
                birds and coyotes, but they usually just
                move deeper into the woods for the time
                being.

MARK: So, you don't think there are any bigger
                predators at all in the park?

RANGER KENDRA: Like what? Ain't no bears and the last
                cougar sighting was years ago…

CHARLIE: Well...

PATTERSON: Go on.

CHARLIE: What about Bigfoot?

                <u>PAUSE.</u>

RANGER KENDRA:Ok, my brother really got to you didn't

                he... Look, kids, I'm gonna put it to you

                bluntly--99% of all injuries I see out

                here are accidents. Bigfoot is not real.

                The only dangerous monsters out here are

                drunk tourists.

CHARLIE: So everything Dr. Von Bron told us is-

RANGER KENDRA:Do you know what kind of doctor he is?

MARK: Ecology?

PATTERSON: Witch doctor.

RANGER KENDRA:Close: he's a doctor of parapsychology. I

                tried to get him into my doctorate

                program-

PATTERSON: You've got a doctorate?

KENDRA: PhD actually. Are you surprised?

CHARLIE: You work in a forest.

RANGER KENDRA:Of course, I work in a forest. Anybody

                smart works in a forest. People are

                stupid. I'd rather be around trees.

MARK: Right. Look, we're looking for our

                friend. He went hiking out here 11 days

                ago and hasn't been seen since.

RANGER KENDRA: Hmm. 11 days ago? Why haven't we had a missing persons report?

PATTERSON: The police told us not to worry about it.

RANGER KENDRA: Really? Well, if your friend is still in the park, I'll bet you anything he did something stupid. Got stuck in some ravine, pissed off the wrong bear, or ate some untoward berries. Something like that.

MARK: So, you think Sasha just tripped and fell?

RANGER KENDRA: Hey I'm sorry, kids. But I have seen a lot of human stupidity in my time as a park ranger.

CHARLIE: That's not Sasha. Your brother said that you could help us.

RANGER KENDRA: And I'm trying. But the reality is that your friend probably brought whatever happened upon himself.

PATTERSON: Sounds about right.

RANGER KENDRA: My brother can spin you all sorts of stories about Bigfoot and whatnot, but the truth is that your friend more than likely had an accident.

MARK: So, in all your years as a park ranger,

                  you've never seen any proof of Bigfoot?

RANGER KENDRA: Nope. And every year… Every year someone

                  gets hurt at that stupid Bigfoot

                  Festival. And then I have to clean up the

                  mess.

CHARLIE: Do you think it would be _more_ dangerous

                  to have the festival this year?

RANGER KENDRA: Do I think the festival is dangerous

                  because Bigfoot's running through the

                  woods attacking your friend? No. Most

                  certainly not. Do I observe increased

                  stupidity every year during the festival?

                  You bet.

                  CUT TAPE.

SCENE 3.

FOOTSTEPS IN FOREST. SILENCE FOR A WHILE,
OCCASIONAL BIRD TWEETS.

MARK: I just don't believe Sasha could have slipped and fallen to his death. It's just so… anticlimactic.

PATTERSON: I mean, it kind of makes sense. Sasha was clumsy.

SILENCE.

PATTERSON: Do you remember the time Sasha knocked over the display at Blue Star?

MARK: (SHORT LAUGH) Doughnuts went everywhere. Hey, but he paid for them. He didn't leave them hanging. The whole team got doughnuts enough to bring home to their kids.

CHARLIE: I saw Sasha knock over a Bigfoot once. My
              aunt got a Bigfoot dummy for the
              festival. One like the famous picture,
              you know, like it's walking, swinging its
              arms, and then looks at the camera. He
              knocked it down the first time she showed
              it to us and its head popped off and
              landed right at her feet.

MARK: Yeah. He was a klutz. But… was he so
              klutzy he could have died? I don't want
              to imagine we lost him just because he
              wasn't paying attention to the path.

PATTERSON: So, what are our alternatives then? A.
              Sasha is so stupid he fell to his death?
              Or B. He was eaten by Bigfoot. Which
              death is more likely?

CHARLIE: But you remember the voicemail. Something
              screamed, then there was a gunshot. Then—
              no more Sasha. That's not an accident,
              unless it was a hunting accident…

              THEY APPROACH TWO VOICES IN THE FOREST.

              BIRDS CHIRP NEARBY.

HANS: There. Do you see it?

FRANZ: Ooh, the eastern whip-poor-will!

HANS: What a find! What a find indeed!

PATTERSON: (WHISPERING) Are those the guys from

                 yesterday?

MARK: (WHISPERING) Those are the guys who said

                 they saw Bigfoot.

CHARLIE: Yep, that's them all right. Come on,

                 let's go say hi. I'll introduce you. Hey

                 Hans. Franz!

HANS: Oh. Oh!

FRANZ: Oh, why hello Charlie.

HANS: And friends! Who are these two strapping

                 lads?

MARK: I'm Mark.

PATTERSON: Patterson.

CHARLIE: They're helping me look for Sasha.

FRANZ: And where is that dashing boy of yours? I

                 don't recall seeing him at the hunt. Did

                 he miss the big show?

MARK: The hunt?

FRANZ: Well not a literal hunt. We're not

                 savages with guns and slaughter and all

                 that. We are-

HANS: (BIRD CALL)

PATTERSON: What the f-

MARK: Was that a bird?

HANS: Indeed it was! The Yellow Footed

                Trillback to be precise.

MARK: Are you birders?

FRANZ: Indeed we are!

HANS: But eventually you see so many horny-

                spotted owls, and then-

FRANZ: And then you crave something bigger.

HANS: We're squatch-ers now.

FRANZ: (BIGFOOT CALL)

HANS: (BIGFOOT CALL)

FRANZ: (BIGFOOT CALL)

HANS & FRANZ: (FUN-HAD-BY-ALL LAUGHTER)

CHARLIE: Uh…

HANS: We like the sense of danger of course,

                it's more exciting than birds.

CHARLIE: And now that you've seen Bigfoot, what's

                next?

HANS: Oh. Well, I hadn't thought of that. Once

                you've seen the Foot, where's left to go?

MARK: (CLEARS THROAT) What did Bigfoot look

                like?

HANS: Well, he was tall and fast.

FRANZ: Yes, like a shadow.

HANS: A wounded shadow.

FRANZ: And oh the sounds he made.

               HANS AND FRANZ APPROXIMATE PATTERSON'S

               SUFFERING.

HANS: It was a harrowing experience to say the

               least.

FRANZ: We would flee the country for safety

               concerns, but well, once you sink your

               teeth into the Foot, you just never let

               go.

HANS: Yes, we're a regular pair of bear traps.

               Haha.

PATTERSON: So-you saw Jacko too. Is that right?

FRANZ: Yes. Precisely. It went like this: First,

               we saw Bigfoot off in the distance.

HANS: With our own eyes.

PATTERSON: How far?

FRANZ: Oh, maybe fifty feet?

PATTERSON: So far?

HANS: Do you want to hear the story or not?

CHARLIE: We'll be quiet. Go on.

FRANZ: And then there were loud footsteps. Jacko

               came running out of the brush.

HANS: Straight at the squatch!

FRANZ: He's quite the terror.

HANS: He raised his gun and…

FRANZ: BANG!

CHARLIE: So he got something?

HANS: Well. That I can't say for certain.

FRANZ: There was so much shouting and shooting.

HANS: It was bedlam!

FRANZ: The squatch disappeared after that. So…

CHARLIE: So he did get it.

HANS: Maybe, maybe.

FRANZ: But there was something very strange…

MARK: What? What was strange?

HANS: Well, admittedly, we saw all of this at
              some distance. But we swear we heard your
              dear aunt Annie chastising poor Jacko.

CHARLIE: What? What did she say?

FRANZ: (UNCOMFORTABLE) I don't think…

CHARLIE: What did you hear?

HANS: We must suggest you go and talk to Jacko
              yourself.

              CUT TAPE.

Episode 6

The Night of the Hunter

IN THE CAR, EDGE OF WOODS, MUSIC.

MARK: So what should we expect?

CHARLIE: What do you mean?

MARK: Well, you know Jacko. How do you expect

he'll take us showing up unannounced?

PATTERSON: Yeah, you think he'll take a shot at us?

CHARLIE: What?! No. He's not like that.

PATTERSON: So he's not the type to go around

shooting things in a city park either?

CHARLIE: I guess that's what we're trying to find

out.

PATTERSON: I guess so.

MARK: So…any advice?

PATTERSON: Don't startle him.

CHARLIE: Actually, yeah. Don't startle him.

MARK: Great, I'll try to remember that.

CHARLIE: And maybe let me do the talking?

MARK: What? Why?

CHARLE: He's my aunt's boyfriend—

PATTERSON: Eww, how old are they?

CHARLIE: How old are you? And he seems to have a
                soft spot for me.

MARK: Oh? How long have you known Jacko?

CHARLIE: Known? Most of my life. He was part of
                the society back when I was a kid. But
                talked to? It's only since I got back a
                couple months ago that he's been willing
                to speak to me.

MARK: He didn't before?

CHARLIE: (LAUGHS) No. He doesn't stand fools
                lightly.

PATTERSON: And you're a fool.

CHARLIE: I _was_ a child.

MARK: So this relationship between him and your
                aunt is new?

CHARLIE: Mm. A few years? It definitely started
                after high school.

MARK: But long enough that they're close.

CHARLIE: Why?

MARK: I just...has your aunt said anything
                about him? Have you asked her if he could
                have had something to do with Sasha?

CHARLIE: I haven't...I mean, she doesn't...

PATTERSON: You didn't ask.

CHARLIE: No.

PATTERSON: Even though he's a creep.

CHARLIE: (DELIBERATE THOUGHT) I'd say he's creep-
                adjacent.

MARK: But you don't think he was involved.

CHARLIE: Do you?

MARK: I don't know.

PATTERSON: Really?

                BLINKER, CAR PULLING ONTO GRAVEL.

MARK: Wait, where are we going?

CHARLIE: He lives way back in the woods. Off the
                grid.

PATTERSON: Nooo, he's not weird at all.

                SILENCE AS THEY DRIVE.

MARK: But what if he's involved?

CHARLIE: What if?

MARK: Are we just going to confront him?

PATTERSON: That's what I was trying to say!

                SILENCE.

CHARLIE: No. I don't think we should do that.

MARK: He's a big man.

PATTERSON: And seems pretty familiar with guns.

CHARLIE: We're just trying to get information.

MARK: A fact finding mission.

PATTERSON: And when we find the facts?

              SILENCE.

CHARLIE: I guess we'll find out.

              BLINKER. CAR PULLS TO A STOP.

              We're here.

SCENE 2.

CAR DOOR SLAMS. FOOTSTEPS ON GRAVEL.

PATTERSON: This place is a dump.

CHARLIE: What'd you expect?

PATTERSON: His rifle's expensive.

MARK: (SARCASTIC) I guess he's got his priorities straight.

FOOTSTEPS ON WOOD AS THEY CLIMB THE PORCH.

CHARLIE: (YELLING) Jacko?

KNOCKING ON THE DOOR.

CHARLIE: (YELLING) Jacko, are ya here? It's Charlie.

MARK: And us.

CHARLIE: Keep quiet, he's not too keen on strangers.

PATTERSON: Now you tell us.

MORE KNOCKING.

CHARLIE: (Yelling) Jacko? Jacko? Are you here?

MARK: Well, now what?

PATTERSON: Hey, it's unlocked.

MARK: And?! You want to break into *this* guy's house?

CHARLIE: Calm down, it's not breaking in.

SOUND OF CHARLIE STEPPING INTO THE CREEPY HOUSE.

MARK: (HISSING) Charlie, come back!

PATTERSON: Stop being such a wuss, Mark. I want to find Sasha. I'm going in.

SOUND OF PATTERSON ENTERING THE HOUSE.

WIND BLOWS THROUGH THE TREE OUTSIDE.

MARK: Shit.

SOUND OF MARK ENTERING THE HOUSE.

Patterson? Charlie? Where are you guys?

CREAKING FLOORBOARDS.

Guys? Stop messing.

SOMETHING CRASHES TO THE FLOOR.

Shit!

PATTERSON: Sorry. Sorry. Just bumped into something.

MARK: Patterson! Be careful man. What the hell is that anyway?

MARK PICKS SOMETHING UP.

PATTERSON: I dunno, an animal skull or something.

MARK: Shit. Who keeps that in their house?

              <u>MARK SETS IT DOWN.</u>

              Have you seen Charlie?

PATTERSON: Nuhuh. She disappeared.

MARK: Shit. Why would she do that?!

PATTERSON: She's nuts.

MARK: I guess.

PATTERSON: You think she's in cahoots with Jacko?

MARK: (CLEARS THROAT) Okay Charlie, come back

              out now.

PATTERSON: So this is the kind of girl Sasha liked.

MARK: Charlie! Come on. Let's just leave.

              Jacko's obviously not here, alright?

              <u>QUICK FOOTSTEPS, BOARD SQUEAK, MARK TURNS</u>

              <u>AROUND.</u>

MARK: (SCARED) Woh, Ok Charlie. Ok. This is

              revenge for pretending to be Sasha. I get

              it. Our bad. We're sorry. Can you come

              out now?

              <u>QUICK FOOTSTEPS, BOARD SQUEAK, MARK TURNS</u>

              <u>AROUND.</u>

PATTERSON: Screw this, man. This chick is crazy. She

                brought us here on purpose. Jacko's gonna

                jump out and slice us up together-

                LOUD THUD THEN MANY QUICK FOOTSTEPS.

MARK: (TERRIFIED) Charlie! ... Charlie... Is

                that... you?

CHARLIE: (WHISPER DIRECTLY INTO MICROPHONE) yes

                MARK & PATTERSON SCREAM.

PATTERSON: Holy shit. Not cool, Charlotte. Not cool.

CHARLIE: (LAUGHS)

MARK: You got us. We deserved that.

CHARLIE: Hell yeah you did! You should have heard

                yourself scream! (IMITATION SCREAM)

MARK: Okay. Okay, Charlie. Now can we just get

                the hell out of here?

PATTERSON: No way. We just got here.

                PATTERSON OPENS UP FRIDGE.

                Oh. He's got a whole fridge fulla meat.

                That's normal.

CHARLIE: He's a hunter. Probably just deer meat.

PATTERSON: Looks like human meat to me.

                PATTERSON CLOSES FRIDGE.

                MARK WALKS OPENS A DRAWER.

MARK: Drawer full of knives.

CHARLIE: Like you'd find in any kitchen.

MARK: My kitchen doesn't have this many knives.

CHARLIE: Aren't you a vegan?

PATTERSON: Hey! Hey guys, I found the basement.

MARK: Hell no.

PATTERSON: Come on, wussy.

MARK: I'm not going down there.

CHARLIE: You'd rather stay up here alone?

MARK: Shit. Fine. Don't leave me alone again.

PATTERSON: Why don't you go first.

MARK: I hate you.

              CREAKY STEPS.

              You guys are coming right? It sucks down

              here.

              MORE STEPS.

              Guys? Are those chains?

              CLINK OF CHAINS RATTLING.

              Shit. No no no no.

CHARLIE: What'd you find?

              CLINKING OF CHAINS IN ANSWER.

PATTERSON: Kinky.

MARK: Let's leave. We need to leave.

CHARLIE: I don't think that's for humans.

PATTERSON: Just for freaks.

CHARLIE: No, I mean like, for butchering.

MARK: Not helping!

CHARLIE: Butchering animals. To hang them from the

              ceiling.

MARK: Definitely not helping.

CHARLIE: It helps the blood drain!

PATTERSON: Whelp. I guess that explains the bucket

              of blood.

MARK: Fuck.

PATTERSON SLAPS METAL TABLE.

PATTERSON: Is this an operating table?

CHARLIE: Probably where he guts his deer.

MARK: (WHIMPERS) Okay. Did we find it? I mean,

              what are we looking for? What constitutes

              evidence? Knives, blood, chains. That

              does it for me.

CLICK OF METAL-ON-METAL AS GUN IS PICKED

UP.

PATTERSON: Is this a gun?

MARK: Shit.

CHARLIE: Put it down, Patterson.

PATTERSON: Why does a hunter need a handgun?

CHARLIE: Put it down.

PATTERSON: Alright, alright.

MARK: (FROM ANOTHER CORNER OF ROOM) Hey! Over
                here. I think I found something.

                <u>FOOTSTEPS.</u>

                There. Do you think that's...?

CHARLIE: Hair?

PATTERSON: Brown hair.

MARK: Sasha's hair?

PATTERSON: It sure looks like it.

CHARLIE: (PANICKING) What the shit?

                <u>COCK OF GUN.</u>

JACKO: This is a Ruger M77. It's made to drop
                grizzlies at 15 feet so I 'spect it'll
                make mincemeat of the three of you before
                you say 'boo.' So explain to me what
                you're doin here so I don't make a mess
                of my basement.

MARK: We… we… we…

JACKO: Shit, son. Spit it out.

PATTERSON: He means that we were.... that we left...

CHARLIE: My aunt sent us!

JACKO: Charlotte is that you?

CHARLIE: Hi Jacko.

JACKO: What are you doing in my basement? Don't
                you know that's dangerous? I mean, shit
                I've got a gun.

CHARLIE: Sorry, Jacko.

JACKO: No. I'm sorry. I heard voices. I thought
                that…well, you're down here in the dark.
                I grabbed my…Oh my god. I could have-- I
                could have-- Excuse me, but I need to sit
                down.

SCENE 3.

JACKO:	Well, ain't this nice. The four of us, sittin' round my living room, sipping iced teas.
PATTERSON:	Yeah…nice.
MARK:	(MUTTERING) At least he put the gun away.
CHARLIE:	Thanks for being so hospitable, Jacko.
JACKO:	Anything for you, Charlotte. I mean, why wouldn't I ingratiate myself with someone I found poking around my basement.
MARK:	Um—
CHARLIE:	Jacko!
JACKO:	I kid, Charlotte. I kid. But you said Annie sent you into my basement? What for?
CHARLIE:	No. We were looking for Sasha.
JACKO:	Is that right? She finally tell you?

CHARLIE: What? No. She didn't send us. We just
              wanted to ask some questions… Jacko, does
              my aunt know something about Sasha?

JACKO: I'm sorry about what's happened to him.
              He seemed like a nice boy. But I can't
              help you.

MARK: You don't know where he is?

JACKO: He's not here, if that's what you mean.

PATTERSON: You did have all that blood down there.

CHARLIE: And hair.

JACKO: You too, Charlotte?

CHARLIE: Sorry.

JACKO: Hm, you saw all that while you were down
              there. Did you happen to notice a couple
              pelts, and a pair of horns?

CHARLIE: We weren't… not exactly…

JACKO: Charlie-I'm a hunter. I hunt. I shoot
              things. I didn't shoot your boyfriend.
              But I do shoot things. Big things.

CHARLIE: Do you know anything about it, Jacko?

JACKO: I-Look, there's something out there in
                those woods, something dangerous. You
                kids, please, for the love of god tell me
                you won't go wandering out there again,
                at least not in the dark. I couldn't
                stand it if something happened to you,
                Charlie.

PATTERSON: That's not a no.

JACKO: I'm afraid I can't help too much. At
                least not until you talk to Annie.
                Actually, if you're headed her way, I
                have a (PAUSE) a gift for her. Just a
                small something, a symbol of our bond
                together. If you could pass it along, I'm
                going to… Well, I'm not coming to town
                for a little while.

CHARLIE: Jacko…

JACKO: Now, if you'll excuse me. I'm sorry, but
                it's been such a long day.

PATTERSON: That's it?!

JACKO: That's right. And, if anyone else but
                Annie so much as slips a finger under
                that bow, I'm gonna make both you
                chuckleheads disappear.

MARK: What?!

JACKO: You all have a good night.

SCENE 4.

MARK: What the hell, Charlie?

CHARLIE: What?

PATTERSON: Dude's a psycho.

CHARLIE: He's not so bad.

PATTERSON: He pointed a gun at our heads!

MARK: And threatened to make us disappear!

CHARLIE: He was joking.

MARK: Well, he's got quite the sense of humor.

CHARLIE: It's fine. He's fine. We're fine.

MARK: I don't feel fine.

RATTLE OF CAR KEYS. ENGINE STARTS. CAR

BEGINS TO DRIVE.

CHARLIE: You'll get over it.

PATTERSON: So, what's in that box?

CHARLIE: I don't know.

PATTERSON: It's probably Sasha's teeth or hair or

             something...

CHARLIE: He said that was elk fur.

PATTERSON: And he was so convincing.

CHARLIE: I don't know. (PAUSE) I don't know I

               don't know I don't know.

               <u>CAR CONTINUES TO DRIVE.</u>

Episode 7

Night at the Museum

SCENE 1.

MARK: Hello listeners. It's September 17th which means that Sasha has been missing for about two weeks now. We've discovered quite a bit about Sasha in that time-

PATTERSON: Including the fact that he had a secret girlfriend.

CHARLIE: Sitting right here.

MARK: We've interviewed all sorts of people from the secret society that he is involved in. Annnd we're no closer to figuring out what happened to him.

PATTERSON: I wouldn't say that.

MARK: Oh?

PATTERSON: Yeah, I think there's an obvious suspect that <u>some</u> of us are choosing to overlook.

MARK: And that would be…

PATTERSON: Jacko.

CHARLIE: No way.

PATTERSON: See?

CHARLIE: No, Jacko wouldn't hurt anybody.

PATTERSON: Sure. The man with a bucket of blood in
              his basement wouldn't hurt anyone.

CHARLIE: He's not like that! He isn't. He's
              just…he's a big sweety.

PATTERSON: A big sweety who pointed a gun at us.

CHARLIE: No he—

MARK: Okay Charlie, if it's not Jacko, who?

CHARLIE: Well…what about Bigfoot?

PATTERSON: Bigfoot?

CHARLIE: Yeah.

PATTERSON: Really?

CHARLIE: Yes. Everyone saw one the night Sasha
              went missing.

PATTERSON: I can't believe we're really talking
              about this.

CHARLIE: It's better than you accusing my uncle.

PATTERSON: So he's your uncle now? Now that he's a
              killer.

MARK: Okay, okay. Before anyone says something
              they'll regret, let's review some facts.
              One: Sasha disappeared in Forest Park the
              night of September 4th on his way to meet
              Charlie.

CHARLIE: Mmhm.

PATTERSON: Jacko was also in the park that night
              with the rest of the Bigfoot Society.

CHARLIE: Who are all excited because they saw a
              squatch running through the woods.

MARK: We found Sasha's phone on Wildwood Trail.
              Did we talk to anyone who was on that
              trail?

CHARLIE: Mmh. No? But there was that scream on the
              voicemail that he left me.

PATTERSON: There was also a gunshot on the
              voicemail. I don't think Bigfoot is known
              for his sharpshooting.

CHARLIE: But the park ranger said that there's
              been a lot of construction around there.
              It could have just been a jack hammer or
              something.

PATTERSON: At night?

CHARLIE: Alright, no. But Doc said that the
              construction could have been driving off
              Bigfoot's prey. One could have gone after
              Sasha.

PATTERSON: Come on, Charlie. Bigfoot's not real.

CHARLIE: Yes he is.

PATTERSON: Really--?

MARK: --Okay! We snooped around Jacko's house
            to see if we could find anything.

CHARLIE: But we didn't.

PATTERSON: We did! We found a fridge full of meat.

CHARLIE: Deer meat.

PATTERSON: You don't know that! And what about those
            chains? Dude's super creepy.

CHARLIE: But not a psycho. Anyway, my aunt likes
            him.

PATTERSON: Because she's totally sane.

CHARLIE: Hey--!

MARK: We didn't find anything conclusive at
            Jacko's house.

PATTERSON: Because he caught us before we could!

CHARLIE: Because there wasn't anything to be
            found.

MARK: And all that together means...

PATTERSON: Nothing.

CHARLIE: Yeah, we've got nothing.

PATTERSON: So if you don't believe it was Jacko...

CHARLIE: Which I don't.

PATTERSON: I was talking to Mark.

CHARLIE: Oh.

PATTERSON: And you don't believe in fairytales.

___

CHARLIE: Hey!

PATTERSON: Who do you think did it?

MARK: Well, first off: I'm not ready to give up

              on Sasha yet. Maybe he's just lost in the

              woods.

PATTERSON: So you _do_ believe in fairytales.

MARK: But, I guess it does feel like a lot of

              my unanswered questions point towards one

              person.

CHARLIE: Who?

MARK: You.

              SILENCE.

CHARLIE: Me?

MARK: Sorry.

CHARLIE: I don't know what to say.

MARK: Well, we never heard about you until

              Sasha disappeared.

CHARLIE: That's not my fault.

MARK: Sasha didn't keep secrets from us.

CHARLIE: Apparently he did. You ever ask yourself

              why he would do that?

MARK: All the time.

CHARLIE: It was because he knew that you would

              freak out.

MARK: He say that?

CHARLIE: He said that you were drifting apart. He
            didn't feel like you understood him
            anymore.

PATTERSON: What wouldn't we understand?

CHARLIE: Me? The Society? He was changing and you
            guys weren't changing with him.

MARK: But he didn't even try!

CHARLIE: I dunno. He needed someone who would
            listen.

MARK: I listened!

CHARLIE: Someone who wouldn't judge. I tried to
            get him to see someone.

PATTERSON: What, like a shrink?

CHARLIE: He wouldn't do it. Too worried about what
            "people" would say.

MARK: What are you saying?

PATTERSON: That Sasha killed himself?

CHARLIE: What?! No. That I was the only one he
            felt comfortable with.

MARK: Yeah, see… I just don't buy it.

CHARLIE: What.

MARK: I just… that wasn't Sasha. He wasn't
             depressed. If anything, it seemed like
             lately he'd been happier than ever.

CHARLIE: Lately like, say the last month? Ever
             since we started dating?

MARK: No! I mean, yeah but not because… I don't
             know. But then you were the one who he
             was meeting in the woods.

CHARLIE: And he never showed.

PATTERSON: So you say.

CHARLIE: He didn't!

MARK: But you're the only one who can verify
             that.

CHARLIE: What about the voicemail?

MARK: What about it?

CHARLIE: His last voicemail was to *me*. He
             literally said that he couldn't wait to
             see me.

PATTERSON: So? That doesn't mean you didn't see him.

MARK: Exactly. Plus, it only confirms that you
             were the last one to hear from him.

CHARLIE: I don't… But... Why would I show it to
             you then? If I killed him, why would I
             have done any of this?

PATTERSON: Maybe you're trying to throw us off your

              scent.

CHARLIE: Really?! What about the scream, then? The

              scream on the voicemail.

MARK: It _could_ have been human.

CHARLIE: No. No. I won't… It wasn't... I know that

              Bigfoot killed Sasha.

PATTERSON: This again?

CHARLIE: Yes. Bigfoot did it and I can prove it.

MARK: How?

CHARLIE: Come to my aunt's house with me. She's a

              collector. She has all sorts of Bigfoot

              stuff.

PATTERSON: I'm ssuuure. "Real" evidence.

CHARLIE: It is real! Fur, prints, DNA,

              everything.

MARK: Charlie.

CHARLIE: No, Mark. Doesn't this make more sense?

              That an animal killed Sasha? Why would I?

              Why would Jacko? I loved Sasha. I wanted

              him to get help. I'm still trying to help

              him. Why would I want to hurt him?

PATTERSON: Mark.

CHARLIE: Shut up Patterson. Just shut up. You

             don't have to believe. Hell, come with me

             and you can grill my aunt all about her

             boyfriend. But just leave me alone.

             <u>SILENCE.</u>

MARK: Okay. We'll come. I'm not saying that I

             believe you but we'll come.

SCENE 2.

<u>WALKING UP TO THE HOUSE.</u>

CHARLIE: So, just a warning, my aunt can be a little… much.

MARK: I think we saw a little of that at the bigfoot meeting.

CHARLIE: Yeah, well. It can put some people off.

PATTERSON: I wouldn't expect anything less from the woman entwined with Jacko.

<u>KEYS IN LOCK. DOOR OPENING.</u>

CHARLIE: (YELLING) Aunty, I'm home! I brought guests!

<u>FOOTSTEPS ENTERING. DOOR CLOSES.</u>

CHARLIE: (YELLING) Aunty? She's probably upstairs. That's where the museum is.

MARK: Museum?

CHARLIE: Well, more like a room full of oddities. But she does get school visits from time to time.

PATTERSON: You bring children here?

CHARLIE: It's not so bad--I grew up here.

             Actually, I think the Society was one of

             the main reasons I got through high

             school.

PATTERSON: You seemed so normal.

CHARLIE: (LAUGHS) Maybe that's why we didn't get

             on. (PAUSE) Anyway, let's head up and see

             what she's gotten herself into.

             FOOTSTEPS ON STAIRS. KNOCKING AT A DOOR.

             DOOR CREAKS OPEN.

CHARLIE: Aunty? Are you there?

             CRASH OF BOXES.

ANNIE: Oh sweet Buddha.

CHARLIE: Everything alright?

ANNIE: Charlie! Good. Grab a dustpan, that was

             the dried guano for the children's tent.

MARK: Dried guano?

ANNIE: You boys, grab the rest of those boxes

             before they fall.

PATTERSON: I'm not going to-

ANNIE: And be careful how you mind them. That's

             the fossil and bone exhibit.

MARK: (SOTTO VOCE) Just do it, Patterson.

             GRUNTING AND TIDYING NOISES.

MARK: What's all this for, Ms. Charleston?

ANNIE: The Equinox Festival.

PATTERSON: The one run by the Bigfoot group?

ANNIE: Who else? Wait a second, weren't you two

              at our last meeting?

CHARLIE: Don't you remember? These are Sasha's

              friends.

ANNIE: Mark, wasn't it? And you're…?

PATTERSON: Patterson. Sasha's brother.

ANNIE: That's right. Well, now that you're here,

              I've got about three thousand pamphlets

              that need folding.

CHARLIE: Actually, we were hoping to look at your

              Bigfoot remnants.

ANNIE: Most of the good stuff is packed away for

              the festival.

PATTERSON: Of course, it is.

ANNIE: But some of the bric a brac is left in

              the back.

CHARLIE: Thanks aunty. This way boys, welcome to

              the Museum of Curios!

PATTERSON: (SNIGGERS) Seriously?

———

112

CHARLIE: Deadly. It's the largest collection of
               artifacts this side of the Canadian
               border.

PATTERSON: Maybe the largest collection of nonsense.

CHARLIE: Well it's more impressive when all set
               up. There's footprints, pictures, even
               little clumps of mud and hair-real DNA.
               Oh and this, this is a small talisman
               made by a group of young people I met
               living off the grid and-

PATTERSON: Which conveniently hasn't been
               authenticated by scientists.

CHARLIE: Von Bron has tried. He says the papers
               can't get through peer review.

PATTERSON: I wonder why.

CHARLIE: Can't you stop being such a killjoy,
               Patterson? Look around, maybe you'll
               learn something. Like-look at that photo,
               my aunt snapped that last year on Mount
               Shasta.

               ANNIE COMES BUSTLING IN.

ANNIE: Charlie, have you seen the vendor list?
              Next Adventure just quit the hiking
              safety instructional that usually starts
              the Grand Hunt.

PATTERSON: This is a fake.

ANNIE: Excuse me?!

PATTERSON: These suits are difficult to move in.
              Look at the way it's pushing out here,
              animal fur can't do that. The person
              doesn't have the top on quite right.
              That's their elbow sticking out through
              the suit.

ANNIE: Not possible. That's the clearest shot
              anyone at the Society has been able to
              get. Jacko was there, he can vouch for
              it.

PATTERSON: Trust me, someone was pulling a prank on
              you.

ANNIE: Hmm. No wonder National Geographic didn't
              accept it.

CHARLIE: Aunty, do you have anything from the hunt
              earlier this month?

ANNIE: What do you mean?

CHARLIE: Everyone at the Society is agog about the
                sighting. Hans and Franz didn't get
                photos, but did you manage to get
                anything?

ANNIE: I didn't see anything during that hunt.

CHARLIE: But everyone saw it!

ANNIE: I didn't. Did you?

CHARLIE: No. I was waiting for Sasha.

ANNIE: And I was with Jacko. Neither of us saw
                anything.

MARK: But he said there was something out
                there...

ANNIE: I don't care what he said. We didn't see
                anything. It was a quiet night.

PATTERSON: Did you hear a gunshot?

ANNIE: There was no gunshot. Nothing happened.
                We had a nice walk in the woods under the
                stars. It was romantic.

CHARLIE: Okay, aunty. We just want to know--

ANNIE: No. I won't take any more of these
                implications. It'll ruin the festival if
                people start going around shouting about
                the dangers of Bigfoot.

MARK: No one mentioned Bigfoot.

ANNIE: He's a gentle soul who wouldn't hurt a
                fly.

PATTERSON: Can you say the same for Jacko?

ANNIE: Excuse you? What are you trying to imply?

CHARLIE: Nothing Aunty. Nobody's trying to say
                anything. Let's just take a breath. We
                went to see Jacko a couple of days ago,
                is all.

ANNIE: Oh yeah?

CHARLIE: Yeah, actually. He sent along a gift for
                you. Here, why don't you open it.

MARK: He seemed like a good guy-

PATTERSON: (SNORTS)

MARK: -And we just got curious. How long have
                you and Jacko been together?

ANNIE: A couple of years.

MARK: And what kind of person is he?

SOUND OF GIFT OPENING.

PATTERSON: Would he hurt someone?

ANNIE: (DISTRACTED) Oh.

CHARLIE: What is it, Aunty?

ANNIE: Nothing. It's nothing.

CHARLIE: What did he send you?

ANNIE: No, nothing. Just a small bauble to show

                his love.

CHARLIE: Ooh! Sounds wonderful. Let's see it.

ANNIE: I'd rather—

                <u>RUSTLE OF WRAPPING PAPER.</u>

CHARLIE: (GASP) That's Sasha's ring.

ANNIE: No its—

MARK: It's a GHS class ring.

ANNIE: I don't think so.

MARK: Green gemstone.

PATTERSON: surrounded by footprints.

CHARLIE: That's Sasha's ring.

Episode 8

Confessions of a Monster Hunter

SCENE 1.

<u>ANNIE'S HOUSE.</u>

CHARLIE: Aunty. Why did Jacko give you this ring?

ANNIE: I don't know. You'll have to ask him.

CHARLIE: Aunty.

MARK: We know that's Sasha's ring.

ANNIE: No, it can't be.

PATTERSON: Even the emerald is chipped.

ANNIE: I don't know anything about that.

CHARLIE: Why did Jacko send you this ring?

ANNIE: I… I don't know.

PATTERSON: Do you know where Sasha's body is?

ANNIE: This must be some sort of mistake.

CHARLIE: Aunty.

ANNIE: It's… it's just a gift from my boyfriend.

CHARLIE: No. It's <u>my</u> boyfriend's ring.

MARK: What happened that night?

ANNIE: What night?

PATTERSON: The night you killed Sasha.

ANNIE: No we didn't--

CHARLIE: The night of the Society's last Bigfoot
              hunt.

ANNIE: I don't recall.

MARK: You were out with Jacko.

ANNIE: No.

CHARLIE: Hans and Franz saw you.

MARK: You separated from the rest of the group.
              And then there was a gunshot.

ANNIE: That wasn't us.

CHARLIE: Aunty, please. You need to help us. Tell
              us what you know.

PATTERSON: You shot Sasha.

ANNIE: No.

PATTERSON: Or Jacko did.

ANNIE: I… I don't know where the ring came from.
              Jacko must have found it in the woods.

CHARLIE: Aunty.

MARK: We just want to know the truth.

ANNIE: I don't know anything.

PATTERSON: Maybe we should ask Jacko.

MARK: What?

PATTERSON: See if their story matches up.

CHARLIE: What story? She says she doesn't know
              anything.

ANNIE: I don't.

PATTERSON: Then Jacko shouldn't either.

ANNIE: I don't know what he knows.

PATTERSON: Let's ask.

CHARLIE: And then what?

PATTERSON: Then we'll find out.

                BEAT.

ANNIE: I can call him.

                BEAT.

ANNIE: Where do you want to meet?

MARK: Some place public. For safety.

ANNIE: I know just the place.

SCENE 2.

<u>STORE BELL AS DOOR OPENS.</u>

<u>DINER NOISES.</u>

WAITRESS: Table for three?

CHARLIE: Four. We're meeting someone.

WAITRESS: Big fella?

PATTERSON: That's right. Kinda scary-like.

WAITRESS: He's over there in the booth. That gonna be enough room?

MARK: We'll squeeze.

<u>FOOTSTEPS.</u>

CHARLIE: Hi Jacko. Thanks for coming.

JACKO: Charlie. Annie. Didn't expect so many of ya.

ANNIE: The kids are a little confused. They want to know what happened that night.

JACKO: Are you recording this?

MARK: We're making a podcast.

JACKO: No way.

ANNIE: Jacko, wait. Just tell them what
                happened. To clear everything up for the
                record.

JACKO: Right… for the record.

CHARLIE: Uncle Jacko, where did you find this
                ring?

                <u>SOUND OF RING BEING SET ON TABLE.</u>

JACKO: Oh… Uh, in the forest.

PATTERSON: Wow. Quite the find.

JACKO: Uh huh.

PATTERSON: When was this?

JACKO: Um...

ANNIE: You found it a couple days ago. That's
                what he told me.

MARK: You said you did know--

JACKO: Yeah, yeah. Couple of days ago. I was out
                with my metal detector.

PATTERSON: It was my brother's ring.

JACKO: Oh.

ANNIE: It's a beautiful ring. If you found it in
                the woods, wouldn't you pick it up?

PATTERSON: Was this before or after the last Bigfoot
                hunt?

JACKO: After.

ANNIE: Of course after. Sasha didn't go missing
              until that night.

PATTERSON: Of course, of course. Can you tell us
              what happened that night?

JACKO: Well, uh. Me and Annie was out with the
              group. But uh, we got separated.

ANNIE: Like I said.

JACKO: Yeah, we stepped away. Thought we heard
              something.

ANNIE: But it was nothing.

JACKO: No, er. Nothing.

PATTERSON: Was this before you shot something?

JACKO: I didn't hit anything.

ANNIE: I told you it wasn't us.

MARK: I heard you shot Bigfoot.

JACKO: What? No. No, I didn't hit him.

ANNIE: We didn't shoot at anything. Must have
              been somebody else.

CHARLIE: Jacko, you're the only one in the Society
              that goes to those events armed.

ANNIE: Plenty of people who live in the woods
              carry guns. Isn't that right, Jacko?

JACKO: Right. Sure. Lot's.

MARK: Okay.

ANNIE: We never saw Sasha.

CHARLIE: But you heard the gunshot.

JACKO: Yes.

ANNIE: No.

CHARLIE: What did you do then?

JACKO: Um, rushed towards it?

PATTERSON: What did you see?

JACKO: I saw… we saw…

ANNIE: It was nothing.

JACKO: It was-

PATTERSON: It was something.

JACKO: Yeah, it was something.

ANNIE: You must be confused. There was a
              gunshot. But we didn't see anything.

CHARLIE: Jacko, what did you shoot?

JACKO: It-

ANNIE: I'm telling you. It couldn't have been
              Jacko. He didn't even have his gun that
              night.

PATTERSON: Who did you shoot, Jacko?

JACKO: It-It was Bigfoot. I shot Bigfoot.

MARK: You shot Bigfoot?

ANNIE: He's mad.

JACKO: I shot Bigfoot. But I had good reason.

PATTERSON: Excuse me?

JACKO: I didn't shoot your brother. I was trying
              to save him.

MARK: What… exactly did you see?

JACKO: Charlie, I'm so sorry.

CHARLIE: What happened, Jacko?

ANNIE: Nothing happened.

JACKO: Your aunt and I were out there, and we
              heard something. Some kind of struggle.
              We ran after it; your aunt and I chased
              the sound.

ANNIE: No. I took no part in this. I didn't do
              anything.

JACKO: You can't hide it anymore. You were
              there. I was there. We saw what we saw.

PATTERSON: What did you see?

JACKO: It was Bigfoot. I couldn't believe it. I
              had finally seen Bigfoot. And he was so
              close. Not a stone's throw away. And
              there was someone with him.

ANNIE: No.

CHARLIE: Jacko. Who was it?

JACKO: I couldn't quite tell. 'Cause Bigfoot was

                holding a rock. A big rock. And before I

                could react, he smashed it down and broke

                the guy's head. The blood. Oh lord, so

                much blood. I took aim and shot. I

                thought I hit it. Bigfoot fell but got

                back up and started running through the

                trees. I couldn't get another shot. It

                ran so fast. God, Charlie. I'm so sorry.

                I'm so, so sorry.

CHARLIE: What then?

ANNIE: Don't say it.

JACKO: We went over to the body. I didn't

                recognize him then, too much blood. But

                your aunt-

ANNIE: No.

JACKO: She checked his pulse. He was gone. I

                wanted to call the police. But she said-

ANNIE: Enough. Enough. I'm not going to let you

                lie anymore.

JACKO: Annie?

ANNIE: No. None of this happened. Bigfoot

                wouldn't do this. I wouldn't do this.

                He's making it all up.

CHARLIE: Aunty.

ANNIE: No, Charlie. I won't listen to it any

                longer. He's the one who shot the poor

                boy. He's the one who buried the body.

                He's the one whose responsible for all of

                it.

PATTERSON: He killed Sasha.

JACKO: No.

ANNIE: Yes. He did. And he's trying to drag me

                down with him.

JACKO: I can't believe you. How can you sit

                there and lie to your own niece like

                that? Especially when you-

ANNIE: Be very careful now, Jacko.

                <u>BEAT</u>.

MARK: What is it?

CHARLIE: What's he talking about, Aunty?

ANNIE: Nothing. Absolutely nothing. Now get up.

                We're going.

JACKO: Are you really going to make me do it?

ANNIE: Its stubbornness making you do it, not

                me.

JACKO: Ok. If that's how it's gonna be. I said

                we'd better call the police. She refused.

ANNIE: Get up, Charlie. Everything he's saying
            is false. You can't sit here and listen
            to this.

CHARLIE: Aunty-

ANNIE: He's trying to ruin everything. If you
            sit here and listen to him it's all gone:
            the festival, the Society, everything.

MARK: I think we know who's telling the truth.

ANNIE: Charlie?

            <u>BEAT.</u>

CHARLIE: What happened next, Jacko?

ANNIE: You've made your choice.

            <u>SOUND OF CHAIR SCRAPING BACK FROM TABLE.</u>

JACKO: Where are you going?

ANNIE: To the police. Someone needs to report
            this. And only I know the truth.

JACKO: Annie, we've run from this long enough.
            They've got us.

ANNIE: No. They've got you. You're the only one
            who's done anything wrong.

            <u>FOOTSTEPS. DINER BELL JINGLES AS ANNIE
            EXITS.</u>

MARK: What happened next?

JACKO: We argued. This is when we really argued.

              Who was going to believe me, she said.

              She said even she didn't believe it, and

              if she didn't believe it the evidence was

              stacked against me. The stone was big. So

              big nobody else could lift it. Just me,

              and maybe some of the football players.

CHARLIE: So you didn't call the police.

JACKO: Your aunt was right. What would I say?

              That I found Sasha murdered in the woods?

              We were the only ones there. I had

              discharged a bullet. My only excuse was

              that Bigfoot did it. I'm sorry Charlie.

              He was already dead. I didn't want to go

              to jail. Your aunt worried that it would

              affect the Society.

CHARLIE: Why didn't you tell me?

JACKO: I didn't know for sure. Not till you
                started poking around with these two. I
                think your aunt knew the whole time. I
                thought it was just some John Doe. I am
                so sorry, Charlie. Your aunt said... I
                thought that- well, if it were some
                drifter, the festival needn't be ruined.
                That wouldn't be good at all. If it was
                just some loner, then who cared. But then
                you three started asking questions…

CHARLIE: So she knew it was Sasha?

JACKO: I can't say for sure. Maybe she did,
                maybe she didn't.

CHARLIE: I can't believe it.

JACKO: Your aunt cares deeply for the Society,
                Charlie. And its soul is the Bigfoot
                festival. If something like this got out,
                if it got out that Bigfoot killed
                someone-

PATTERSON: Or that you killed someone.

JACKO: But I didn't kill anybody.

PATTERSON: You really expect us to believe that
               Bigfoot killed someone, only two people
               witnessed it, and one of those two blames
               you.

JACKO: I told you I didn't do it. It was
               Bigfoot.

PATTERSON: Bigfoot... really...

JACKO: I saw him. It was him.

PATTERSON: Really.

JACKO: The whole society was in those woods.
               They can vouch for me.

CHARLIE: I'm not so sure they will.

SCENE 3.

<u>THE STUDIO.</u>

MARK: Wow. That was… wow.

PATTERSON: I can't believe I… they confessed.

MARK: Yeah. Straight up. (BEAT) Charlie?

CHARLIE: Still here.

PATTERSON: Still think Bigfoot did it?

CHARLIE: I don't… That wasn't a confession.

PATTERSON: Come on!

CHARLIE: Jacko said that Bigfoot did it.

PATTERSON: And your aunt said that Jacko did!

CHARLIE: I… I guess.

MARK: Charlie, don't you think we should tell

            someone about this?

CHARLIE: I don't know.

PATTERSON: Coward.

MARK: Patterson! (TO CHARLIE) This is what

            we've been looking for. We know what

            happened to Sasha.

CHARLIE: I guess.

MARK: So now we need to do the next part.

CHARLIE: I… you're right.

MARK: Do you want me to?

CHARLIE: No… I will.

                 <u>PHONE DIALING. RINGING.</u>

DET. MOSBLEY: Portland Police Department, Detective

                 Mosbly Speaking.

CHARLIE: Hello? I'd like to report a murder.

Episode 9

The Festival

SCENE 1.

MARK: So… to our listeners, some of you might
            have been surprised to see this episode
            drop today, what with last week's…
            climax. Truth is, while this podcast
            started out as a literal cry for help,
            it's become a way for us to process… all
            of this. Now that we've found the end of
            Sasha's story, we felt like we needed one
            more chance to talk about it.

            SILENCE.

            Charlie do you wanna...?

CHARLIE: No.

MARK: Okay, but we're trying to-

CHARLIE: I don't want to talk about it.

MARK: Okay. Patterson?

PATTERSON: What's there to say?

MARK: I don't know. How does it make you feel
            knowing that we caught Sasha's killer?

PATTERSON: Damn good.

               BEAT.

MARK: Care to explain?

PATTERSON: What do you want? It feels

               great...locking up bad guys and doing the

               right thing.

CHARLIE: They're not bad guys.

PATTERSON: What?

CHARLIE: She's not a bad guy.

PATTERSON: You're the one who called the cops.

CHARLIE: I… I know.

PATTERSON: Your aunt and that lunatic Jacko, killed

               Sasha.

MARK: Patterson, Stop.

PATTERSON: Stop?! Mark! Annie killed Sasha.

CHARLIE: I know.

PATTERSON: Then you should be ashamed to call her

               family.

MARK: Enough! Too far Patterson.

PATTERSON: It is not too far! That evil bitch killed

               my brother and now Charlie's defending

               her.

CHARLIE: I… I'm not. I can't anymore. I'm done.

               CHARLIE STANDS TO LEAVE.

MARK: Come on, Charlie. Just wait—

CHARLIE: (AWAY FROM MIC) See you at the festival.

              FOOTSTEPS. DOOR CLOSES.

MARK: Really, Patterson?

PATTERSON: What? I said what I said.

MARK: It was cruel.

PATTERSON: It wasn't cruel. It was honest.

MARK: No it—

PATTERSON: (INTERRUPTING) It was Charlie that

              dragged Sasha into this. It was Charlie

              he went to meet in the woods. And it was

              her aunt that murdered him. She's the one

              to blame for this.

              LONG SILENCE.

MARK: It's shit like this that makes me

              understand why Sasha kept secrets from

              us.

PATTERSON: No. It's Charlie. It's that cult. And you

              want to ignore all of it. You think

              they're a bunch of eccentrics playing

              fairytale but actually they're

              dangerous.

MARK: I just want to talk to them. They were
               the ones that Sasha felt at home with. I
               want answers.

PATTERSON: Answers?! Mark—Jacko murdered Sasha. Case
               closed.

MARK: I- Maybe. I just. There's something
               missing. It doesn't feel right.

PATTERSON: You've got to be kidding me.

MARK: There's just something that doesn't sit
               right. When I looked into Jacko's eyes, I
               think he was being honest.

PATTERSON: Are you serious? Bigfoot isn't real,
               Mark. These people are all deluded. You
               can't- Wait a minute. You dog. I know
               what this is. You just want another shot
               at Charlie, don't you.

MARK: What? No.

PATTERSON: You've been keeping her so close this
               whole time. You want-

MARK: No. That's not it at all. There's just
               something that's not clicking for me. His
               death. It just feels so random. There
               must be something that someone at Bigfoot
               Society knows that we're not seeing.

PATTERSON: They're a bunch of loons who killed him.

MARK: Not the ones who are left. And they were
              all out in the woods that night. Maybe
              one of them saw Jacko or Annie.

PATTERSON: Huh.

MARK: I just… I miss him. I want to know what
              he saw in them. What we weren't able to
              give him. I feel like I'm still letting
              him down.

PATTERSON: No, he let us down. If he needed, he
              could have talked to us.

MARK: No. No. If I were… If he felt like he
              could share stuff, like Charlie-why did
              he keep her a secret?

PATTERSON: Because he was wrapped around her little
              finger. And he died because of it.

MARK: I should have known he was in trouble. If
              I had paid attention, maybe he would
              still be here.

PATTERSON: No, you'd be dead too.

MARK: What?

PATTERSON: Maybe those psychos would have killed you
              too.

MARK: No. He wouldn't have been alone that

                night. He wouldn't have needed to sneak

                around with Charlie.

PATTERSON: (SIGH) If you insist on talking with her

                and the other psychos, I'll come with

                you.

MARK: Go with me…

PATTERSON: To the festival. You're right, we need to

                make sure that none of the others saw

                anything that night. But I swear, if you

                start believing it's Bigfoot, I'm out.

                I'm done.

                PHONE RINGS.

PATTERSON: Shit. Hold on. (TO PHONE) Hello?

DET. MOSBLEY: This is the PPD. Is this Patterson

                Ketchum?

PATTERSON: This is. What's this about?

DET. MOSBLEY: We may have located your brother, Sasha.

PATTERSON: Really? How did you find him?

DET. MOSBLEY: A hiker in the park. We need you to come

                identify the body.

PATTERSON: Oh. Okay then. I guess I'll be in

               shortly. See you. (TO MARK) That was the

               police.

MARK: What? What did they want?

PATTERSON: They found Sasha.

MARK: Really?! Where is he? Is he alright?

PATTERSON: They want us to come in and identify the

               body.

MARK: Oh. Right.

SCENE 2.

PATTERSON: Hello?

PAUSE--NO ANSWER.

Is there anyone here?

FOOTSTEPS.

MARK: HELLO?

DR. RAHUL: (CHIPPER) Welcome to Multnomah County
             Medical Examiners. My name is Doctor
             Rahul Chakrabarti, lead medical examiner.
             How can I help you this fine day?

MARK: We're here to I.D. our friend.

DR. RAHUL: Right. Of course. Um, my condolences?

             PAUSE.

             What's their name?

MARK: Sasha Ketchum.

DR. RAHUL: Ah! The John Doe found in the park
             yesterday. The detective is here to see
             you. One moment.

<u>FOOTSTEPS. A DOOR.</u>

(OFF) Detective? They're here.

<u>FOOTSTEPS.</u>

DET. MOSBLEY: Hello boys. Thank you for coming in.

PATTERSON: I didn't know you'd be here.

DET. MOSBLEY: Standard practice to have someone here for the I.D.

MARK: (DISTRACTED) Are you going to be the one to show us...?

DET. MOSBLEY: No, the doctor will be taking care of that. I'm just here for support. Doctor? Lead the way.

DR. RAHUL: Perfect! Follow me.

<u>FOOTSTEPS DOWN ECHOING CORRIDOR</u>

<u>(THROUGHOUT NEXT DIALOGUE).</u>

PATTERSON: Can you tell us how he was found?

DET. MOSBLEY: A hiker literally stumbled over the corpse. It seems that it had been half buried.

MARK: Buried?

DET. MOSBLEY: Yes. This lines up with the information that we garnered from our primary suspect.

PATTERSON: You mean Jacko.

DET. MOSBLEY: Technically I'm not supposed to talk
                about active investigations.

                But since you turned him in... Yes, Mr.
                Jacko's story lines up with where and how
                the body was found.

MARK: So you believe him.

DET. MOSBLEY: Well...

PATTERSON: You think Bigfoot is the murderer?!

DET. MOSBLEY: No. No, of course not. The truth in _parts_
                of Mr. Jacko's story has only further
                solidified his involvement in the crime.

PATTERSON: Good.

DR. RAHUL: Here we are! If you could all just step
                back for a moment.

                FREEZER DOOR OPENS. METAL GURNEY ROLLS
                OUT.

MARK: Is that him?

DET. MOSBLEY: That's what I hope you'll tell me.

DR. RAHUL: Before I pull back the sheet, I should
                probably warn you: it's not going to be
                pretty.

PATTERSON: We get it, he's dead.

DR. RAHUL: Yes, he's dead. But he perished from a

                massive head injury. I just don't want

                you to faint at the sight of brains.

PATTERSON: Brains?!

MARK: Wait. Is there a bullet wound? We heard

                someone was shot.

DR. RAHUL: A gunshot? Oh no, no, no. Not a bullet

                wound on him. This was most definitely

                blunt force trauma.

DET. MOSBLEY: Who do you think was shot?

MARK: I don't… I thought…

PATTERSON: Jacko was lying.

MARK: He said he shot Bigfoot.

PATTERSON: I think Jacko _was_ Bigfoot.

DET. MOSBLEY: Boys. Let's not get distracted by a mad

                man's ravings.

PATTERSON: No. We're just- It's been a long day.

MARK: You're quite sure it wasn't a gunshot?

DR. RAHUL: Quite sure. It was definitely a large

                blow to the head. Or blood loss. But in

                my experience anytime you can see pink

                stuff, 1 quick. I need to show you the

                body now. Do you think you can handle

                this?

MARK: (SIMULTANEOUS) No.

PATTERSON: (SIMULTANEOUS) Yes.

                SOUND OF FABRIC BEING PULLED BACK.

                LONG PAUSE.

MARK: That's him.

DET. MOSBLEY: Are you sure?

MARK: Yes. That's Sasha.

DR. RAHUL: Okay, perfect!

                FABRIC IS PUT BACK. GURNEY IS RETURNED.

                FREEZER IS CLOSED. FOOTSTEPS BACK DOWN

                THE HALL.

MARK: That's it? Do you need another statement

                or something?

DET. MOSBLEY: No. The I.D. is enough. Unless there's

                anything else you can think of?

MARK: Um...

PATTERSON: No.

DET. MOSBLEY: Are you sure? We need to have a rock-

                solid case against this guy.

PATTERSON: We already told you everything we know.

DET. MOSBLEY: Alright. You know where to find me.

MARK: Thank you, detective.

DR. RAHUL: Have a wonderful day!

                DOOR. OUTSIDE NOISES. SILENCE.

PATTERSON: You're quiet.

MARK: Yeah. That was...

PATTERSON: Yeah.

              <u>SILENCE.</u>

PATTERSON: What now?

MARK: I dunno. The festival?

PATTERSON: Really?

MARK: It could be a good distraction.

PATTERSON: Yeah.

SCENE 3.

<u>OUTDOOR AT THE FESTIVAL. SOUND OF BANJO</u>

<u>BEING PLAYED IN THE DISTANCE AND GENERAL</u>

<u>CROWDS.</u>

MARK: Does it feel weird being back here?

PATTERSON: What do you mean?

MARK: Forest Park. Where Sasha died.

PATTERSON: It's a big park.

MARK: And Sasha could have been found anywhere.

             I mean, what if he died over there by the

             food carts? Or over by the children's

             games? They could be playing hide and

             seek right where he died.

PATTERSON: We're a long way from where we found his

             phone. Anyway, I wouldn't worry about

             that. It's a party--just try to enjoy

             yourself.

MARK: Yeah...

PATTERSON: Hey, you want a beer? I see a booth.

             Maybe it'll help you relax a little.

MARK: (DISTRACTED) I can't believe he's gone.

PATTERSON: (SNAPPING HIS FINGERS) Hey, hey. Beer.

               I'm getting you some. Snap out of it.

MARK: Al-Alright, yeah sure.

               PATTERSON RECEDES INTO THE CROWD. MARK

               WALKS ALONE FOR A BIT BEFORE A CHANT

               FILTERS OUT OF THE CROWD.

CORY: Whose got big feet?

CROWD: (WEAKLY) We've got big feet.

CORY: Whose got big feet?!

CROWD: We've got big...

               GENERAL CROWD NOISES AS EVERYONE HAS

               LEFT.

CORY: Aww man... Hey! Don't I know you.

MARK: What? Hey, yeah. I'm Mark. You're- you're

               the school mascot. Cory, right?

CORY: Yessir! I mean, no sir! Today I'm Sassy

               the Sasquatch, reporting for duty.

MARK: Still haven't found the suit I see.

CORY: Man, no way. She's gone. I think someone

               must have stolen her.

MARK: That sucks.

CORY: Yeah, and you should see my brother. He's
               almost bald! Not sure what I'm going to
               do...

MARK: Buy a new suit?

CORY: You know how expensive those things are?
               No way the school pays for it. Anyway,
               they're trying to blame me. Said I
               shouldn't have taken it off at the game
               three weeks ago.

MARK: Do they want you to sleep in it?

CORY: I dunno, man. But they say I owe them a
               thousand bucks.

MARK: Shit.

CORY: I was only out of it for a minute! Needed
               to use the booster's private office.

MARK: The what?

CORY: You know, the secret bathroom the
               boosters use.

MARK: They don't.

CORY: They do! They got it when they donated
               the Jumbotron. Anyway, I set it on the
               sofa while I was in the stall and it
               vanished.

MARK: They have a sofa in the bathroom?

CORY: Sofa, flatscreen, it even live-streams
               the game.

MARK: Crazy.

CORY: Oh yeah. What else would you expect from
               a bunch of richie-rich alumni wanting to
               relive their glory days? They've got a
               trophy stand and everything.

<u>PATTERSON'S VOICE EMERGES FROM OUT OF THE
CROWD.</u>

PATTERSON: (OFF) Yeah, same to you buddy. Mark,
               look, I got us beers, but these people
               are insane. I don't- Oh- hello.

CORY: Mr. Ketchum!

PATTERSON: Cory? What are you doing here?

CORY: They ask me to work it every year. It's
               always full of crazies so I usually turn
               them down, but now I need the cash. So I
               called them last week to see if they
               still wanted me.

MARK: That's something.

CORY: I thought so. The woman in charge agreed,

             even with the missing suit. But now the

             new kooks in charge won't pay. When I

             showed up they said they'd only payout if

             I could draw a big enough crowd.

MARK: New kooks?

CORY: Some guys, Hans and Franz? Really off the

             wall.

MARK: They're in charge?

PATTERSON: Of course. They replace one murderess

             with two crackpots.

MARK: Well, good luck with everything.

CORY: Thanks! It was good seeing you Mr.

             Ketchum!

PATTERSON: You too, kid.

CORY: Gooo Bigfoots!

             AS MARK AND PATTERSON MOVE ON, CORY CAN

             BE HEARD BEGINNING ONE OF THEIR CHANTS.

MARK: Crazy who you run into at these things.

PATTERSON: Yeah, I wouldn't blame him for getting

             high during this one.

MARK: You never told me about the booster's

             secret bathroom.

PATTERSON: What?

MARK: Cory was just saying that his suit
              disappeared from the booster's secret
              bathroom.

PATTERSON: So? It's no big secret. We do a lot for
              the school. Makes sense we'd get
              something in return. Why do you even
              care?

MARK: Dunno. Just found it odd. Wait-Charlie!
              Hey Charlie!

CHARLIE: Oh. Hi, Mark. Patterson.

PATTERSON: Charlie.

              BEAT.

MARK: So, how are you enjoying the festival?

CHARLIE: It's been better.

MARK: Yeah?

CHARLIE: Yeah. When I was a kid I used to run this
              thing. My aunt and I would... It was my
              favorite day of the year.

              AWKWARD SILENCE.

CHARLIE: Anyway, you do anything fun yet? Agatha
              gives killer tarot readings and the
              tracking booth gives out good tips before
              the grand hunt.

PATTERSON: We just got here.

CHARLIE: Oh.

              <u>SILENCE.</u>

MARK: Grand hunt?

CHARLIE: Yeah, it's like the culmination of the
              festival. Everyone goes out into the
              woods to try and spot bigfoot. Someone
              always finds tracks. Though I swear
              Jacko-- or, ah, someone goes out
              beforehand and fakes them for the kids.

MARK: Sounds fun.

CHARLIE: It is.

PATTERSON: Everyone here is going out in the woods?

CHARLIE: Yeah, then we all come back to the shady
              stage for dancing and campfire tales.

PATTERSON: There's been a murder. Is it really a
              good idea? The woods. In the dark?

CHARLIE: What's the matter? Afraid of the dark?

PATTERSON: What? No. It just doesn't seem like a
              good idea.

CHARLIE: I thought the culprits were in jail,
              right? We should all be celebrating.

MARK: Charlie…

CHARLIE: Sorry.

PATTERSON: Give it up, Mark.

MARK: Patterson, please.

PATTERSON: Charlie's still making excuses for her
               psycho family. Why can't you see it?

MARK: Fuck you, Patterson.

PATTERSON: You've bought into this whole fantasy,
               Mark. I told you she was involved, right
               from the beginning. Charlie's aunt killed
               Sasha. And you're taking her side. I-
               (CLEARS THROAT) Look, I said I'd leave if
               you started to believe. Well, I'm out.
               Don't come running to me when you find
               yourself staring down the barrel of
               Jacko's gun.

               FOOTSTEPS FADE INTO THE CROWD.

SCENE 4.

THE GRAND HUNT.

CROWD NOISE.

HANS: (THROUGH A MIC) Hello everyone!

FRANZ: (THROUGH A MIC) And welcome to the
            seventy-third annual Bigfoot Society's
            Fall Equinox Festival!

CHEERS FROM THE CROWD!

HANS: We are the Festival's interim
            coordinators, Hans!

FRANZ: And Franz!

HANS: And while we could spend hours thanking
            all the non-murderous people who made
            this Festival happen--

FRANZ: We'd rather you go out and enjoy
            yourself!

HANS: So, before we send you off into the woods
            to conduct the Grand Hunt, we'd like to
            introduce a special guest to go over some
            ground rules with you.

FRANZ: Please put your hands together to welcome
                Ranger Kendra of the Portland Parks
                Department.

                CLAPPING AND CHEERS.

                KENDRA BUMPS THE MIC AND CAUSES A LITTLE

                FEEDBACK.

RANGER KENDRA:Um, hello. I'm Ranger Kendra and I'm only
                here as a last-minute favor for my little
                brother. He said that, whether I approved
                or not, you would all be wandering into
                the woods. So I'm here to make sure that
                you don't get lost or end up dead. Now a
                couple rules: first don't leave the path.
                Now, my brother has insisted that you
                will be leaving the path. It's unsafe and
                unadvised and you will likely get hurt.
                Now, if you do decide to ignore my
                warning and leave the path, only do so
                with a buddy. That way if you run into
                any wild animals, they will get double
                the meal and be less likely to come after
                the rest of us...That was a joke.

Since there are so many of you intent on going off the path, make sure that you and your buddy are always within earshot of the other hoodlums. If you do get lost, utilize your safety whistles and someone will come find you. That leads me to rule number five: bring a safety whistle. If you don't have one, I'm sure the fine and totally sane coordinators of this event will be able to provide you with one. If you utilize your whistle and it seems like no one is coming for you, and this is really important, do not try to get unlost. You are much more likely to run further into the deep dark woods. Instead, if you want to be rescued, stay in one place. Keep blowing that whistle and someone will eventually find you.

THE FOLLOWING DIALOGUE HAPPENS OVER THE TOP OF KENDRA'S MONOLOGUE, WITH KENDRA FADING IN AND OUT AT APPROPRIATE TIMES.

MARK: Sorry about earlier. With Patterson.

CHARLIE: Whatever.

MARK: I feel like I'm always apologizing for
           him.

CHARLIE: Yeah. Why do you do it?

MARK: Apologize? I guess I've always done it.

CHARLIE: But why do you put up with him?

MARK: I dunno. I guess he's always been around.
           It was me and Sasha and him. And now with
           Sasha gone…

           <u>BEAT.</u>

MARK: I think he'd really want to be here
           today.

CHARLIE: He'd love it.

           <u>BEAT.</u>

           I saw her, you know.

MARK: What?

CHARLIE: My Aunt. I went to the jail. Right before
           I came here. She still insists they
           didn't do it. Now she claims it was
           Bigfoot.

MARK: Like Jacko said.

CHARLIE: Yeah.

MARK: And?

CHARLIE: And what?

MARK: Do you believe her?

CHARLIE: Do you? Do you think Bigfoot killed

              Sasha?

              <u>BEAT.</u>

MARK: No.

CHARLIE: No one else will either.

MARK: But do you?

              <u>SILENCE.</u>

              <u>END KENDRA'S MONOLOGUE.</u>

KENDRA: So, since I can't talk any of you out of

              it, good luck I guess. Try not to get

              eaten.

HANS: Thank you Kendra for that stirring

              speech!

FRANZ: Now, good luck!

HANS: Happy hunting!

FRANZ & HANS: And spot that Squatch! (BIGFOOT CALLS!)

Episode 10

Into the Woods

SCENE 1.

THE GRAND HUNT.

CROWD NOISE.

FRANZ: Good luck!

HANS: Happy hunting!

FRANZ & HANS: And spot that Squatch! (BIGFOOT CALLS!)

CROWD NOISES.

CHARLIE: Well, shall we?

MARK: Are you sure?

CHARLIE: Come on. Let's try to have a little fun.

CROWD NOISES. FOOTSTEPS.

CROWD NOISES BEGIN TO DISSIPATE AS FOREST

SOUNDS INCREASE.

MARK: It is nice out here, away from the

crowds.

CHARLIE: Yeah, that's half the reason I love the

Society. We're always getting out into

nature.

MARK: What's the other half?

CHARLIE: The thrill of finding Bigfoot, of course.

MARK: Of course.

               <u>FOOTSTEPS & FOREST NOISES ONLY.</u>

MARK: What was Sasha's reason?

CHARLIE: For the Society? He loved Bigfoot.

MARK: So he _was_ a true believer?

CHARLIE: I think so. But it was more than that.
               For the first time, I think he was
               beginning to realize that he could
               choose.

MARK: Choose what?

CHARLIE: Life, I guess? That he wasn't stuck being
               the same person he had been in high
               school.

MARK: That he didn't have to have the same
               friends?

CHARLIE: Yeah, he could like what he wanted to
               like. That there were people out there
               who wouldn't just put up with him but
               actually wanted to engage with him.

MARK: I can see that.

CHARLIE: Look at the Society. As much as they
               fight, as much as they're crazy, everyone
               there looks out for one another.

MARK: It's a family.

CHARLIE: Exactly. That's what Sasha was looking
              for.

MARK: And that's what Patterson and I weren't
              giving him.

              <u>BEAT.</u>

CHARLIE: I don't know.

              <u>SILENCE.</u>

CHARLIE: About Patterson…

MARK: He's…not a huge fan of the Society. Or
              you.

CHARLIE: (SARCASTIC) You don't say.

              <u>BEAT.</u>

              I'm glad he's not here.

MARK: He's not always been this bad.

CHARLIE: That's not how I remember it.

MARK: What do you mean?

CHARLIE: He was an asshole back when we were
              together. Maybe moreso. At least, he had
              a harder time trying to hide it.

MARK: I thought you only went on a couple of
              dates?

CHARLIE: Yeah, three or four. And then he
                got…possessive. He forbade me from
                talking to other boys. Even about school
                stuff.

MARK: Yikes.

CHARLIE: That's why we broke up. He was just so
                intense. I almost didn't give Sasha a
                shot because of it. Because how much
                different from his brother could he
                actually be? But, you know, that was high
                school. You give people a second chance,
                especially after high school.

MARK: And Patterson's second chance?

CHARLIE: What do you think?

                <u>SILENCE.</u>

CHARLIE: You know, I was supposed to meet Sasha
                pretty close to here that night.

MARK: Yeah?

CHARLIE: Yeah. Just over that ridge, the hill
                gives way to a stream. We had a spot on
                an old oak that fell across the water.

MARK: Sounds nice.

CHARLIE: It is.

                <u>BEAT.</u>

<hr>

166

Do you want to see it?

MARK: Sure.

<u>SILENCE.</u>

MARK: I still don't get what happened that

             night.

CHARLIE: What do you mean?

MARK: Your aunt says Bigfoot killed Sasha but

             the whole Society heard Jacko fire his

             gun.

CHARLIE: Yeah.

MARK: But Sasha wasn't shot.

CHARLIE: What?

MARK: I went to the morgue. Sasha was…his head

             was crushed by something big.

CHARLIE: Wait, what? Like a rock?

MARK: Exactly like a rock.

CHARLIE: But that's what Jacko said!

MARK: I know.

CHARLIE: Don't you see what that means?

MARK: What?

CHARLIE: They're being framed!

MARK: I don't know…

CHARLIE: Mark, you have to believe me! Jacko's a
            good shot. He wouldn't need to use a
            rock.

MARK: So, who did it?

CHARLIE: There's only one person who makes sense-
            Bigfoot!

MARK: Charlie…

CHARLIE: Why won't you believe me, Mark? It's what
            all the evidence points to.

MARK: Bigfoot is framing your aunt? Listen to
            yourself, Charlie. I agree that the
            evidence doesn't line up. But, Bigfoot?

CHARLIE: Sasha would have believed it.
            <u>SILENCE.</u>

MARK: I don't know what to believe.

SCENE 2.

169

<u>RUSTLING IN THE BRUSH.</u>

MARK: (WHISPERING) Wait, Charlie. I think
             there's someone over there.

CHARLIE: What?

<u>FOOTSTEPS PAUSE.</u>

<u>PATTERSON STRUGGLING WITH SOMETHING.</u>

CHARLIE: Oh my god, is that .. Patterson? What's
             he doing?

<u>MORE MOVEMENT & STRUGGLE.</u>

MARK: Hey Patterson, are you alright?

PATTERSON: Shit! Hey, you scared the daylights out
             of me.

CHARLIE: What are you doing out here?

PATTERSON: Um, looking for Bigfoot-same as you.

MARK: I thought you were an animal!

PATTERSON: Haha, no. Just someone getting lost in
             the woods.

MARK: I thought you left?

PATTERSON: I was going to. But…look, I'm sorry for
                what I said. I wanted to make sure you
                were safe out here.

CHARLIE: We were just headed down to the stream.

PATTERSON: Oh. I've already looked over there. No
                Bigfoot in sight.

CHARLIE: Actually, I wanted to show Mark where I
                was going to meet Sasha.

PATTERSON: Is that around here?

MARK: Why are you covered in dirt, Patterson?

PATTERSON: Um, I was…I was following you.

CHARLIE: And why would you do that?

PATTERSON: Because…I don't trust you with Mark.

CHARLIE: Surprise, surprise.

PATTERSON: You're going to get him killed out here,
                just like you did with Sasha.

MARK: Hey, guys.

CHARLIE: Seriously?! That's what you're worried
                about?

PATTERSON: Yeah, that's what I'm worried about. Come
                on Mark, let's leave this psycho to her
                games.

MARK: Guys, stop.

CHARLIE: What is with you?! Ever since the soccer
               game, you've been trying to accuse me of
               murder.

PATTERSON: And I was right! You're the reason Sasha
               was killed out here!

MARK: Guys! What is that?

PATTERSON: It's nothing.

CHARLIE: Is that-Is that a body?

               <u>SILENCE.</u>

PATTERSON: I think it's some debris. A trick of the
               light.

MARK: Patterson, what were you doing out here?

PATTERSON: I told you-I'm protecting you, Mark.

MARK: Move, Patterson.

PATTERSON: No.

CHARLIE: Why not?

PATTERSON: I just can't.

               <u>FOOTSTEPS.</u>

PATTERSON: Stop. Mark. Don't get any closer.

MARK: It's under all that leaves and dirt but
               it looks...

CHARLIE: Furry?

PATTERSON: You need to get away.

MARK: Yeah, furry. Like...

CHARLIE: Bigfoot?

MARK: No way.

CHARLIE: Yes it totally does look like Bigfoot.

MARK: I don't believe it.

PATTERSON: Wow. Look, we found Bigfoot.

CHARLIE: Did you kill it?

PATTERSON: What? No. Let's go get the others.

                They're not going to believe this.

MARK: I'm gonna touch it.

PATTERSON: Don't-It could be dangerous!

BRUSH SOUNDS AS MARK POKES BIGFOOT.

MARK: Oh.

CHARLIE: What?

MARK: It's empty.

CHARLIE: What?

MARK: It's a suit. It's empty.

PATTERSON: Shit.

MARK: I think it's the missing mascot suit.

CHARLIE: What's it doing out here?

PATTERSON: I have no idea.

MARK: Patterson, help me pull it out.

PATTERSON: I can't--uh, my arm.

CHARLIE: Let me.

GRUNTS AS SUIT IS PULLED OUT.

CHARLIE: It's definitely the mascot suit.

MARK: I don't understand. Cory said it

              disappeared from the Booster's bathroom

              at the school.

CHARLIE: Well, whoever took it obviously was

              trying to get rid of it.

MARK: Look: the arm's coming off.

CHARLIE: Is that a… bullet hole?

PATTERSON: Shit.

              <u>SILENCE.</u>

MARK: Jacko did shoot Bigfoot that night. Or at

              least someone who was dressed like

              Bigfoot.

PATTERSON: I don't know...

MARK: It would have to be someone with access

              to the Booster's club.

CHARLIE: Someone who knew that Sasha was coming

              out here that night.

PATTERSON: It's Cory's suit. Maybe Cory's lying

              about it disappearing. Maybe that's why

              he's here today.

MARK: Yeah?

PATTERSON: Sure. He's obviously involved in this

               cult. Probably got caught up in the

               psychosis.

MARK: He said that he usually avoids these

               events. Just signed up for this one

               recently.

PATTERSON: Exactly! Trying to cover his tracks.

MARK: Would he even know who Sasha was?

CHARLIE: Patterson, how did you hurt your arm

               again?

PATTERSON: I fell down the stairs.

MARK: Let me see.

PATTERSON: No.

               MARK GRUNTS. THERE'S A TUSSLE. PATTERSON

               IS PAINED.

MARK: That's a bullet wound.

PATTERSON: Fuck off.

CHARLIE: You did it.

PATTERSON: Shut up.

CHARLIE: You killed Sasha.

PATTERSON: I said shut up.

MARK: Patterson.

PATTERSON: Oh, go blow it out your butthole, Mark.
                Yes, I killed Sasha. I kind of wish I
                killed you now too.

MARK: Why?

PATTERSON: Cause you're a sanctimonious asshole.

CHARLIE: Why did you kill Sasha?

PATTERSON: Because of you! He told me about your
                stupid little Society. He told me that he
                met you and that you slept with him. You
                were _my_ girlfriend.

CHARLIE: No.

PATTERSON: He had no right! And then he stopped
                hanging around. Was too busy for his own
                brother.

MARK: Patterson.

PATTERSON: What an asshole! I tried to talk to him.
                Tried to explain. But he just wanted to
                spend time with you.

MARK: Enough, Patterson.

PATTERSON: No! Surely you see, Mark. Everything's
                better without him. We're together. We're
                actually spending time together. Going to
                games and festivals, making a podcast--

MARK: We were trying to find Sasha!

PATTERSON: So? We were doing it together!

MARK: Because you killed him!

PATTERSON: It's better this way! Sasha was pulling

              away from us.

MARK: You strung us along.

PATTERSON: I planted his phone a long way from here.

              I wanted you to see the truth. He was

              done with us.

CHARLIE: But my aunt.

PATTERSON: Got in the way. They saw me. Took a shot

              at me. Tried to stop me.

CHARLIE: They were protecting Sasha.

PATTERSON: He didn't deserve it. You can see that,

              right? He was going to throw us away.

CHARLIE: No he wasn't.

PATTERSON: He'd throw you away too. Eventually.

              We're all better without him.

CHARLIE: Not my aunt. Not Jacko.

PATTERSON: They're idiots. Hid the body for me. Took

              care of everything.

MARK: Except the suit.

PATTERSON: Except the suit with my blood.

MARK: But you buried it.

PATTERSON: That night. I took it off the path where
              I knew it wouldn't be found.

CHARLIE: Until you found out that the Society
              would be all over these woods.

PATTERSON: Fucking Society.

MARK: So now what?

PATTERSON: Now? Now we go home. Pretend we don't
              know. Maybe bury the suit better. Let's
              go home, Mark.

MARK: Fuck you, Patterson.

PATTERSON: I wish you'd just listen for once.

              <u>GUN IS DRAWN AND COCKED.</u>

CHARLIE: Patterson, what are you doing?

PATTERSON: Scary, isn't it? It's Jacko's. I took it
              the night we broke into his house. Hell,
              I wish I had found it sooner. Would have
              saved me a lot of grief.

MARK: You don't have to do this, Patterson.

PATTERSON: I kinda think I do, Mark. Give me your
              phone. I know you're recording.

MARK: Please don't do this.

              <u>PHONE CHANGES HANDS</u>

CHARLIE: You're not going to get away with this,

                Patterson. There's tons of people out

                here.

PATTERSON: And not one member of your sacred Society

                is going to save you. How does it feel to

                be all alone at the end, Charlie. Do you

                think this is how Sasha felt?

MARK: Asshole.

                MARK PUNCHES PATTERSON. THERE'S A

                SCUFFLE. SCREAMING AND YELLING FROM ALL

PATTERSON: Get off, Mark!

                GUN GOES OFF. SCREAMS.

CHARLIE: Mark! Are you hurt?

                FOOTBEATS RUNNING. PATTERSON'S BREATH

                PUFFING.

MARK: (DISTANT) No. Where'd he go?

PATTERSON: Fuck. Fuck, fuck, fuck.

                MORE RUNNING.

                I think I lost them. Fuck. What now? What

                now?

                MORE RUNNING.

                Where do I go? Where do I... FUCK!

                PUFFING OF BREATH FADES. QUIET OF

                FOREST.

<u>A STREAM.</u>

I don't know. I don't know. Oh fuck. I'm fucked.

<u>SPLASHING IN WATER.</u>

I need to make it back. Steal a car. Then what?

<u>TWIG SNAPS.</u>

Hello?

<u>SILENCE.</u>

Hello? Who's there? You should know that I'm really dangerous. I killed somebody. Hello?

<u>SILENCE.</u>

Oh fuck.

<u>HEAVY FOOTSTEPS.</u>

FUCK.

<u>RUNNING. HEAVY FOOTSTEPS FOLLOWING.</u>

<u>AN ANIMALISTIC SCREAM. PATTERSON SCREAMS.</u>

<u>PHONE IS DROPPED.</u>

<u>HEAVY FOOTSTEPS DRAGGING A BODY AWAY.</u>

<u>SILENCE.</u>

The Bigfoot Society
Published by Deep Overstock
www.portlandparanormalpodcast.com

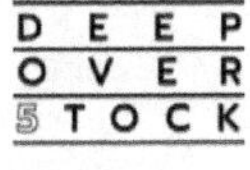

Cover art by Viviann Ruiz